MISSION SURVIVAL

SANDS OF THE SCORPION

www.randomhousechildrens.co.uk

CHARACTER PROFILES

Beck Granger

At just thirteen years old, Beck Granger knows more about the art of survival than most military experts learn in a lifetime. When he was young he travelled with his parents to some of the most remote places in the world, from Antarctica to the African Bush, and he picked up many vital survival skills from the remote tribes he met along the way.

Uncle Al

Professor Sir Alan Granger is one of the world's most respected anthropologists. His stint as a judge on a reality television show made him a household name, but to Beck he will always be plain old Uncle Al – more comfortable in his lab with a microscope than hob-nobbing with the rich and famous. He believes that patience is a virtue and has a 'never-say-die' attitude to life. For the past few years he has been acting as guardian to Beck, who has come to think of him as a second father.

David & Melanie Granger

Beck's mum and dad were Special Operations Directors for the environmental direct action group, Green Force. Together with Beck, they spent time with remote tribes in some of the world's most extreme places. Several years ago their light plane mysteriously crashed in the jungle. Their bodies were never found and the cause of the accident remains unknown . . .

Peter Grey

Beck's best friend from school may not be much to look at, but his small and slim figure belies a boy who is brave, determined and only occasionally stubborn. Having known Beck for many years, the two have a firm bond in spite of their constant bickering. He is rarely to be seen without his pride and joy – the digital camera he got for his birthday.

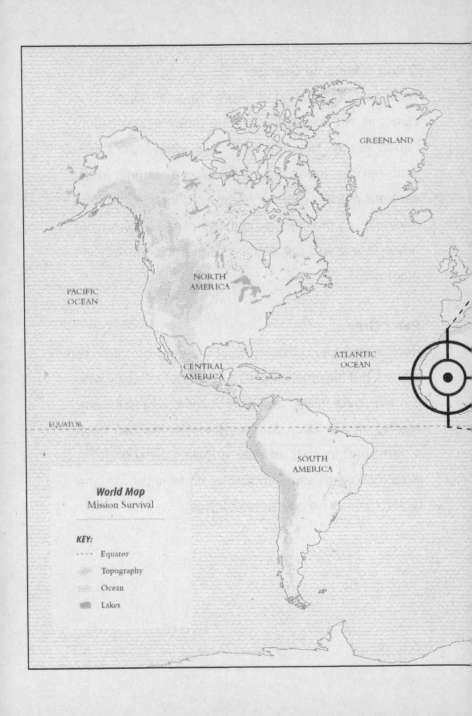

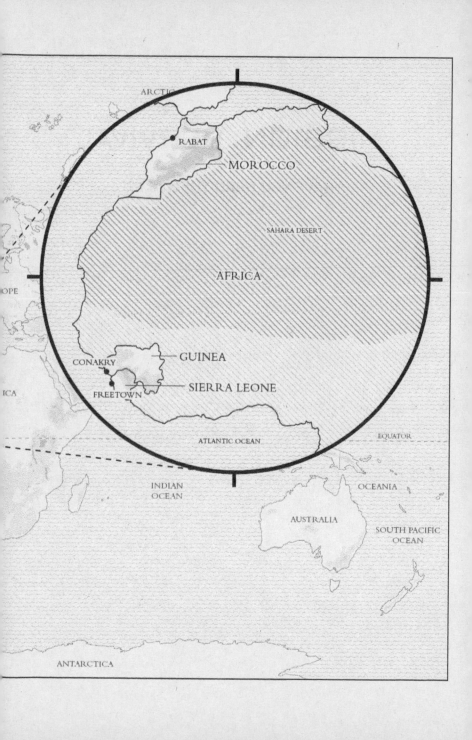

MISSION SURVIVAL

HAVE YOU READ THEM ALL?

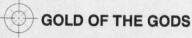

GOLD OF THE GODS

Location: The Colombian Jungle

Dangers: Snakes; starvation; howler monkeys

Beck travels to Colombia in search of the legendary City of Gold. Could a mysterious amulet provide the key to uncovering a secret that was thought to be lost forever?

WAY OF THE WOLF

Location: The Alaskan Mountains

Dangers: Snow storms; wolves; white-water rapids

After his plane crashes in the Alaskan wilderness, Beck has to stave off hunger and the cold as he treks through the frozen mountains in search of help.

SANDS OF THE SCORPION

Location: The Sahara Desert

Dangers: Diamond smugglers; heatstroke; scorpions

Beck is forced into the Sahara Desert to escape a gang of diamond smugglers. Can he survive the heat and evade the smugglers as he makes his way back to safety?

 TRACKS OF THE TIGER

Location: The Indonesian Wilderness

Dangers: Volcanoes; tigers; orang-utans

When a volcanic eruption strands him in the jungles of Indonesia, Beck must test his survival skills against red-hot lava, a gang of illegal loggers, and the tigers that are on his trail . . .

CLAWS OF THE CROCODILE

Location: The Australian Outback

Dangers: Flash floods; salt-water crocodiles; deadly radiation

Beck heads to the Outback in search of the truth about the plane crash that killed his parents. But somebody wants the secret to remain hidden – and they will kill to protect it.

SANDS OF THE SCORPION
A RED FOX BOOK 978 1 862 30482 6

First published in Great Britain by Red Fox
an imprint of Random House Children's Publishers UK
A Random House Group Company

First published in Red Fox, 2009
This edition published 2013

17

Penguin Random House is committed to a sustainable future for
our business, our readers and our planet. This book is made from
Forest Stewardship Council® certified paper.

MIX
Paper from
responsible sources
FSC® C018179

Set in Swiss 721 BT

RANDOM HOUSE CHILDREN'S PUBLISHERS UK
61–63 Uxbridge Road, London W5 5SA

www.randomhousechildrens.co.uk
www.randomhouse.co.uk

Addresses for companies within The Random House Group Limited can be found at:
www.randomhouse.co.uk/offices.htm

THE RANDOM HOUSE GROUP Limited Reg. No. 954009

A CIP catalogue record for this book is available from the British Library.

Printed and bound in the UK by Clays Ltd, St Ives plc

MISSION SURVIVAL

SANDS OF THE SCORPION

BEAR GRYLLS

RED FOX

To my youngest son, Huckleberry.
Completing the most gorgeous
trio of young musketeers!
I adore you.
Love
Papa x

CHAPTER 1

The wheels of the plane thumped down on the runway tarmac. Beck Granger lurched forward in his seat as the brakes bit. The plane shook and its engines roared in reverse. Then abruptly the sound died down and he could sit back again while it turned and trundled onto the taxiway.

Beck breathed out quietly. After his recent adventures in Alaska, air travel still made him more nervous than it should.

Across the aisle his Uncle Al smiled and raised an eyebrow. He knew exactly what was going through Beck's mind. The same crash that had made Beck so nervous had almost killed *him* as well. Beck met his eyes and raised an eyebrow in return.

His friend Peter Grey sat in the window seat on his left. They had pulled the blind down over the window to block out the bright sun during the flight.

'Hey, let's see!'

Peter had flipped up the blind before Beck could stop him. The harsh light of Sierra Leone flooded into the cabin.

'Aargh!'

Peter pulled the blind back down quickly, then flashed a bashful grin at Beck. His eyes were wide behind his round glasses. 'Well, we're here!'

'Yup,' Beck agreed.

'Hold on . . .'

Peter opened his bag and rummaged around in it. Beck rolled his eyes as his friend emerged with his pride and joy, the top-of-the-range digital camera he had got for his birthday. It took photos and filmed video equally well. Peter cautiously pushed the blind up again, not so far this time, and pressed the camera against the window.

'*Look, Mummy,*' Beck said in a high, breathless voice, '*I took a photo of yet another airport terminal*

2

and it looked exactly like every other airport terminal I've ever been to!'

'You're just jealous,' Peter said loftily. He slid the camera into a pouch that was clipped to his belt.

Beck smiled.

They had always bickered. Peter was Beck's oldest friend from school; he was small and slim and looked as though, if the wind blew hard, it might knock him over.

That was probably why older boys had tried to pick on him during their first days at school together. A group of teenage bullies twice Peter's size had tried to make him hand over the money in his pocket. They had expected him to be a pushover. What they hadn't expected was that Peter would just say no. He didn't cower. He didn't run away. He didn't fight back. He just refused, and kept on refusing. He simply would not be frightened by the group crowding round him.

Beck had watched in fascination, ready to intervene on Peter's side if it got violent. It became even more fascinating when he worked out what was going on. After five minutes of attempted intimidation he had realized that Peter was playing with them. He had got them to a point where they were telling him what they needed the money for. They had stopped trying to frighten him. Now he was just showing them up as the morons they were, and they were too dim to understand it.

More and more boys had gathered round to watch. Finally the bullies realized, in the dim recesses of their tiny minds, that half the junior school were laughing at them. They left Peter alone after that.

Peter didn't look much, but Beck recognized that he was brave and determined – and sometimes simply stubborn.

The plane had now come to a standstill and the cabin doors were opened. Warm, humid air flooded in to do battle with the plane's air conditioning. The forty-odd passengers clambered to their feet, picked up their bags and shuffled out into the equatorial sunshine.

* * *

The three of them – Beck, Peter and Al, or Professor Sir Alan Granger as he was better known – had flown from London to Freetown, Sierra Leone's capital.

Then they had boarded this smaller plane to fly up country, near to the border with Guinea.

Al was attending a conference on African tribal peoples. They used traditional methods of sustenance that had kept their societies going for thousands of years. The western world had all but forgotten how to farm sustainably. The purpose of the conference was to see what could be learned from these ancient methods.

Al had taken Beck, of course, because he took Beck everywhere. After Beck's parents had disappeared in that fatal plane crash when he was so young, Al had taken the boy in and raised him like a son.

As for Peter, his parents had recently had another baby. He referred to his new little sister as 'The Bundle'. Beck knew he kept a photo of the baby in his wallet, so he was probably much fonder of her than he let on.

'The Bundle' had been born prematurely and was still quite weak, so the Greys hadn't been able to take their usual summer holiday this year. Peter's parents were advised not to do any travelling with her for the time being. So Beck had invited Peter along on this trip too – he would enjoy the company while Al was ensconced in the conference centre and talking to tribal leaders.

After that, the three of them planned to travel up to Morocco for a real holiday.

*   *   *

It wasn't a big modern airport. There was no tunnel from the plane to take them straight into the terminal. They had to walk down some steps and head out across the tarmac, squinting in the sunlight.

It was the first time they had spent any time outdoors since leaving London. Beck took a deep breath of African air. A hot, dry wind blew on his face. It came from the northeast. He worked out the direction by pointing the hour hand of his watch at the sun: halfway between that and twelve o'clock would be south. They were still in the northern hemisphere, he remembered; the direction-finding technique would be accurate. Beck realized that the wind came from the Sahara, only a few hundred miles away.

The Sahara covered a quarter of the African continent. It was vast – almost as big as all of the

USA. The air Beck was breathing had blown across some of the driest land on the planet. It was cooling down now that it had reached the savannah of Sierra Leone's border country, but it still carried a harsh message. It warned that there was a large part of the continent where only the very foolish or the very brave would venture. Or, Beck thought, the very wise – the ones who really knew how to survive there. People like the Berbers, the Tuareg, the Bedouin, who lived and breathed the desert life as naturally as Beck would cross the road back home.

Well, the closest Beck planned to come to the Sahara was when they flew over it en route to Morocco.

CHAPTER TWO

Peter stumbled into Beck. 'Oops! Sorry!'

He had his camera out again and was panning it around the airport. He had been walking backwards and hadn't seen Beck standing there.

'Just taking some pics of the plane,' he added, by way of explanation.

Beck grinned and looked back. 'Yeah, well, it got us here. That's all I really ask a plane to do.'

Peter suddenly flushed red. 'Hey, I'm sorry. I wasn't thinking.'

Beck frowned. 'Huh?'

'I mean, you and' – Peter gestured – 'planes. You know . . .'

Beck smiled knowingly. Peter was referring to his recent Alaskan adventure, which had started with a plane crash. After that it had turned into a trek that included fording a freezing river, crawling over an icy crevasse in a glacier, and spending the night in a snow hole in the mountains while a blizzard raged outside and tried to kill him.

The enquiry into the crash had put it down to failure of the plane's single engine.

'I'm fine with planes,' he insisted – but couldn't resist adding, 'as long as they've got more than one engine. I count 'em carefully before I get on nowadays.'

Peter wasn't quite sure how he was meant to react to that, but when he saw Beck grinning, he relaxed into a laugh.

They collected their bags and emerged into the chaos of the town.

A battered old shuttle bus carried them to their hotel. Beck reckoned it was at least as old as he was: splits in the seats were covered up with rough tape and it lurched from side to side as the driver navigated the traffic, one hand permanently clamped down on the horn. Judging by the din, every other driver seemed to take the same approach.

The roads were packed – mostly with equally battered trucks and lorries, and the occasional gleaming new Jeep or Land Cruiser. This was a culture where, if you had wealth, it was obvious. And there were taxis, hundreds of them, threading their way between the other cars with suicidal ease. Every driver seemed to regard other road users as potential enemies.

There was no air con. The windows were wide open and the spicy, dry air blew through the cabin. It couldn't quite get rid of the smell of stuffy, hot vehicle.

Beck loved it. What was the point of being abroad, he often thought, if you tried to make it exactly like home? The only way to enjoy a town in Africa was to treat it like a town in Africa. Just soak it all in.

He glanced over at Peter and wondered what he made of it. His friend had never been outside Europe before. He chuckled to himself. Peter, of course, was leaning out of the window with his camera pressed to his eye. He seemed to be loving it.

*   *   *

'Hey! A fan!'

It was the first thing Peter said when they stepped into their hotel room. A large three-bladed ceiling fan hummed lazily in the warm air. The room had twin beds and a bathroom off to one side. Gauze curtains billowed gently in the open windows. They filtered the harsh sunlight and helped keep out the insects.

'And a minibar!' Peter checked the cabinet and his face only fell a little. 'Locked.' He ran over to the windows and found a door out to the balcony. He fought his way past the curtains. 'Cool – and a *swimming pool*!'

Beck still hadn't got further than the door. 'And a friend left with both suitcases . . .' he muttered quietly.

He lugged the cases into the room and dropped his own on the bed nearest the window. If Peter wasn't going to make his own choice, he decided, then *he* would.

There was a simple room-service menu on the table between the two beds. Beck picked it up and scanned it quickly. 'No, sorry,' he called. 'This just won't do. We're moving.'

Peter was back inside in a flash. 'We've got to move?' he asked in surprise.

Beck brandished the menu. 'You know there's not a single insect on this? It won't be a holiday without some sort of survival food,' he said with a deadpan expression.

It took Peter a moment to work out he was being wound up. He loved hearing about everything Beck had had to eat on his Alaskan adventure. 'Oh, ha ha! But, c'mon. Look at the pool!'

Beck let his friend pull him out onto the balcony to look at a grassy lawn ringed with weary-looking palm trees and a swimming pool nestled in the middle. It sparkled with clear blue water. The din of the town was blocked out by the bulk of the building. The garden was peaceful, and the pool looked cool and inviting.

'OK,' he agreed. 'Last one in's a sissy . . .'

* * *

'Beck, Peter,' said Al, raising his voice slightly over the restaurant's background chatter, 'this is our hostess, Mrs Chalobah.'

The open-air restaurant was in an adjacent

courtyard. The air was pleasantly cool at this time of day. Candles burned on the tables to ward off insects, and the smells of spicy food drifted on the breeze. The bow-tied waiter had led them through the tables to where Mrs Chalobah, the conference organizer, was already seated. Although Beck had heard plenty about this lady, he had never met her. Now she rose to greet them. She wore brightly coloured robes and headdress and a huge beam on her face.

'Alan! So good to see you!'

Mrs Chalobah kissed Al on both cheeks, and then turned her wide African smile onto the two boys. They shifted slightly uncomfortably: Al had made them dress up in jackets and ties. Beck hoped that it was the only time he would have to wear them on the entire holiday.

'My, two such handsome young men! Here, sit down. Tell me all about your journey . . .'

If she had asked Beck, he would have said something simple like 'Fine, thank you. We got on an aeroplane and we flew to Freetown.' He had met adults who were able to chat endlessly about nothing but he had never mastered the art.

But she had been looking at Peter. Peter could describe the flight from Heathrow as if it was the first flight ever from London to Sierra Leone. He talked, and she encouraged him along with smiles and nods. Beck and Al exchanged looks. Al winked. Beck was warming to Mrs Chalobah.

Then he heard Peter's innocent question:

'Is Mr Chalobah coming tonight?'

Beck saw his uncle wince and guessed it was not the question to ask. Mrs Chalobah's cheerful expression faltered a little.

'Mr Chalobah will not be joining us.' She said it with a simple, sad dignity. Even Peter noticed that there was more to be said – she was just finding the right words. He kept quiet and let her continue at her own pace.

'One of the many problems our country faces is that there are people who would take its wealth to use for their own ends. My husband believed that the money from our diamond industry should be used to bring benefit to Sierra Leone. We are a developing country and that development must be paid for somehow! But' – she sighed – 'there are those – ruthless, wicked people – who take what does not belong to them, make themselves rich, leaving the rest of us to struggle in the dirt.'

'Do you mean smugglers?' Beck asked.

She glanced at him, and nodded with a grave bow of her head. 'I mean smugglers,' she confirmed. 'They are the scourge of this country.'

'Mr Chalobah was a judge . . .' Al began.

'He was a judge,' she said, still with that quiet dignity, 'who sentenced one of the worst of these smugglers to thirty years in jail and confiscated his stolen wealth. His associates took revenge. A thousand mourners came to my husband's funeral, from all walks of life. Friends, complete strangers, even some criminals he had previously sentenced for other crimes – but all united in their contempt for his murderers and their respect for a good man.'

She looked each of them earnestly in the eye. 'Peter, Beck . . . these people I speak of are not nice people at all. They shame the people of Africa. And they are well organized. Their web of evil spreads over the entire continent, and beyond. But with the help of people like your uncle' – she squeezed Al's hand, and suddenly her good mood was back – 'who is a very nice person, and with the help of this conference, hopefully we can make progress and leave these dark times behind us once and for all.'

They all raised their glasses – wine for Mrs Chalobah and Al, fresh fruit juice for the boys – and together they drank a toast to the future.

CHAPTER THREE

The next day the delegates started arriving for the conference. Beck and Peter saw Al briefly at breakfast.

'Got to go,' he said, draining his coffee and standing up. He fumbled for his wallet and pressed some banknotes and coins into Beck's hand. 'Here. In case you need anything. I'll meet you this evening. Bye!'

And after that they were on their own.

Beck had learned that the currency of Sierra Leone was called the leone; Al had left them with the equivalent of about fifty pounds. They investigated some leaflets in the hotel lobby, but they had to admit that the small town in up-country Sierra Leone wasn't really geared up for the tourist trade.

'Fifty quid would be great if we were in London or Paris or New York,' Peter said thoughtfully. He looked sadly at the handful of flyers. 'Not really that many sights to see. Can't wait till we get to Morocco for the real holiday . . .'

'We could collect coins off the bottom of the pool,' Beck suggested with a grin. He swam like a fish and could easily dive down three metres to the floor of the deep end. Peter could barely make it six inches below the surface, but he had spent a lot of the previous day trying.

Peter smiled back. 'Race you!'

* * *

And so the boys spent the morning in the pool. Beck showed Peter how to jack-knife his body on the surface so that his head was pointing straight down and his legs sticking straight up.

'And that way,' he explained as he demonstrated for the umpteenth time, 'you just slide down . . .'

Beck kicked his legs into the air and glided down to the bottom of the pool, retrieving several leone coins he had thrown in. The water roared in his ears and he kicked his way back up to the surface. 'Go on, try it again . . .'

The merest drop of water up his nose made Peter feel like he was drowning. He would invariably convulse and splash about like a break-dancing whale before he emerged, gasping for breath. But finally he was able to convince himself he could do it. After so many attempts that they had both lost count, Peter's fingers finally brushed the bottom of the deep end and grasped a coin.

'I did it!' he shouted triumphantly as his head broke the surface again. 'I did it!'

He just keeps going, Beck thought. *He just keeps on trying*. He was proud of his friend.

After that Peter got out of the pool and filmed Beck diving from as many different angles as he could think of. He tried to film him swimming a length of the pool underwater, but the sun sparkled off the surface so brightly that Beck didn't actually show up on the video. It looked like Peter had filmed up and down an empty pool for a minute.

'I think I've got enough . . .' he said eventually.

He examined the skin of his forearm. 'And I think I'm burning.'

'Didn't you put on any of your sun cream?'

'Yeah, but it probably all washed off in the pool. Dad always says the moment it starts happening I should get out of the sun.' He gave Beck a smile. 'Look, I'm going to try taking some other shots inside.'

'OK. I'll be out in a minute.' Beck somersaulted into the water and disappeared beneath the surface.

He kicked his way up and down the pool but eventually he decided he should get out too. He was very glad he had the kind of skin that didn't burn easily, but this was Africa. He lay down on a lounger beneath a large sunshade and let the warm air dry him naturally. The sun was just a bright glowing light through the cloth above him and he could look at it directly.

It was strange, Beck thought. The sun's warmth gave life to the planet. Without it the Earth would be just a frozen ice-ball. Even when he had been stuck up on an Alaskan mountain, the sun had still, almost imperceptibly, been keeping him warm.

In England it had been a record-breakingly wet summer. They had been grateful for any sun at all. It wasn't hard to see why ancient peoples had worshipped it.

But the sun could wear out its welcome very easily. As a young boy, Beck had been taught by the San bushmen of the Kalahari Desert in southern Africa, and by Aboriginals in the Australian Outback. He had been taken there by his parents, who had worked for the environmental direct action group Green Force. He had learned to have a very healthy respect for the sun. These desert peoples knew that it could kill you in no time at all. In hours, in fact, if you got it wrong.

Beck sighed and stretched. His fingers brushed against a magazine that another guest had left on the table next to him. He picked it up idly. It was a glossy nature magazine, and when it fell open a giant scorpion glared out at him.

The colour photograph spread across two pages. The creature was a light brownish yellow in colour and it looked to Beck like bits of different insects had been sewn together to make a completely new one. The crab-like claws – spread out as if to snatch the reader into its embrace – were as wide as the scorpion was long. The spider-like legs, pointing in the wrong direction, as if the scorpion was as mobile backwards as it was forwards. And the sting . . . Well, the sting of a scorpion. There was nothing else quite like it. It was like a sharp bulbous thorn at the end of the scorpion's tail, glistening with a drop of venom, hanging there like water from a leaky tap. The tail was broken into four or five segments, each almost as thick as the body. It curved up and forwards so that the scorpion could grab its prey with those claws and then jab it to death.

Beneath one of the claws was some text.

Most species of scorpion reach between five and eight centimetres in length, and despite their fearsome appearance, their sting is no more dangerous or harmful than a bee's. The exception to both these rules is the Saharan yellow fat-tailed scorpion (Androctonus australis). It averages ten centimetres in length and is quite possibly the

most venomous scorpion in the world. Almost as
toxic as a cobra's, its sting can lead to paralysis,
convulsions, cardiac arrest or respiratory failure.
The species ranges across the deserts of North
Africa.

Beck raised his eyebrows at the creature. 'I'll remember not to mess with you—' he murmured.

'Beck! *Beck!*'

His friend's voice broke into his thoughts and he looked up. Peter was crouched beside him, glancing anxiously from side to side. He was properly dressed again in a long-sleeved shirt, trousers and wide-brimmed hat, skin all safely covered up.

'Hi, Pete. What's up?'

'Shh!' Peter looked around one more time, and leaned down so that only Beck could hear him. Whatever was bothering him, he obviously thought it was important. 'Get yourself—'

'You know, if you're trying not to make yourself obvious, you're failing big time,' Beck pointed out, smiling. 'Grab this sun lounger beside me. Be a bit more subtle.'

'I'm serious!' Peter hissed through his teeth. 'Look, just get yourself dry and come up to our room. I've got something I need to show you.'

* * *

They sat side by side on Peter's bed and gazed at the screen of his camera. He had his finger on the fast-forward button so that the footage of Beck in the pool whizzed by. He flew into the air and creamed through the water like a torpedo.

'Look,' said Peter.

The footage slowed down. Now it was shots Beck hadn't seen, the ones Peter had taken on his own. There were people milling about in the lobby. Some looked directly at the camera, saw the eager boy filming them, and smiled. There were other shots out of their window, looking down at the pool. Somehow Peter had found a window on the other side of the building, overlooking the street and the daily traffic chaos.

And then there was a small butterfly. It was a translucent blue, clinging to a twig somewhere – it was impossible to identify the background. At first Beck thought it was just a photo but then he noticed the body quiver slightly. He was impressed. Peter had been filming it. He had got right in close without scaring it off.

'OK,' Beck said, 'you've got a future with the BBC Natural History Unit.'

'Not that.' Peter thumbed the volume control, turning it up to maximum. 'Listen.'

Beck leaned closer to the tiny speaker. In the background you could hear a faint voice. A man's voice.

But with the sound turned up like that, every other noise picked up by the camera's microphone was also magnified. Beck could only hear snatches above the background racket.

'. . . product . . . along the path . . .'

Then there was the voice of another man:

'. . . being loaded now . . . clearance . . .'

'. . . papers fixed . . . can't afford . . .'

And, most intriguing of all:

'. . . disguised as . . .'

'Disguised as what?' Beck said, trying to replay the clip. After straining to hear the recording, his own voice sounded very loud.

'I don't know!' Peter replied.

'Where did you get this, anyway?'

'You know those pot plants in the lobby? That's where the butterfly was. But the plants are right next to these pillars. You know, leading out to the courtyard. The guys were standing behind them. I don't think they knew I was there. Listen again.'

They ran through the footage once more. Then they looked at each other.

'Beck . . .' Peter looked around the room nervously, even though they were alone behind a locked door and no one was going to intrude. 'They talked about fixing papers – you know, import papers? And clearance? Customs clearance? And this product is disguised as something?'

Beck's face tightened with concentration.

'Beck,' Peter whispered emphatically, every part of him quivering with excitement, 'you remember what Mrs Chalobah said? I think they're smugglers!'

CHAPTER FOUR

Beck held the serious, earnest gaze. He could tell Peter was really into this: he wanted to be a reporter and here was his very first story.

But there was a pressure building up inside Beck and he couldn't fight it. He tried, but it kept growing and growing. He felt the corners of his mouth twitch. He pressed his lips together to keep them straight but he couldn't stop them.

And then he looked at Peter's face and saw that something similar was happening to his friend too. His shoulders began to shake, and then he just *had* to let it out – a torrent of laughter. Peter broke out into a fit of nervous giggles that turned into laughter of his own. Beck doubled up and Peter fell backwards onto his bed, his chest heaving.

'Smugglers!' Beck gasped. 'Yeah, right!'

He had no idea who the guys actually were or what they had been talking about. He *did* know that proving anything took a lot more than a barely heard conversation and two active imaginations. The chances were that the guys in the lobby were talking about something completely different.

'You have to admit, it would have been kind of cool . . .' Peter tried to continue, but he was laughing too much.

'*Hey, Uncle Al, we've just busted a gang of diamond smugglers—*'

'Tcha!' Peter rolled his eyes and deepened his voice in an imitation of Beck's uncle: '*I just can't leave you alone for a second, can I, boys?*'

Beck straightened up again, still smiling. But his smile dimmed a little when he remembered what Mrs Chalobah had said. If it really had been smugglers, they would have had to tread very, very carefully: probably tell Al, so he could tell Mrs Chalobah, and then get the heck out of Sierra Leone. Let the authorities deal with it. As Al liked to say, let everyone stick to what they're good at.

Someone knocked and they both jumped.

'Boys?' said a familiar voice, muffled by the door. 'You in there?'

Beck went to let his uncle in.

'Hello. There's a break before the delegates' next session so I thought I'd check that you're both OK— What?' he added suspiciously. Both boys were still beaming broadly.

'Nothing,' Beck assured him. 'Yeah, everything's fine. Isn't it, Peter?'

*   *   *

The three of them had dinner together that evening, and breakfast the next morning. But the boys didn't mention anything to Al. He had to leave them again for the final morning of the conference.

Peter and Beck wandered through the lobby, heading back to their room. One of the lifts gave a soft *ding* as its doors slid open.

Peter suddenly pulled Beck over to one side. There was a small, dim passage off the lobby that led to some offices, and that was where Peter had dragged him.

'It's them again!' he hissed. 'The guys I heard

talking! They just got out of the lift.' He nudged Beck forward again. 'Look!'

Beck poked his head round the corner. Two men stood in front of the lifts. They looked to Beck like a perfectly normal pair of guys. One African, one maybe European or American. They were dressed casually – just like a pair of tourists.

The men began to walk towards the entrance, which would take them past the end of their passage. Beck withdrew and Peter pulled him further down the passage.

'So what?' Beck said, tiring of Peter's melodrama.

'I wonder what they're doing . . .'

'I dunno. Maybe they're here for the conference.'

'If they were going to the conference, they'd be in suits or tribal dress like all the others,' Peter pointed out.

'So they're tourists,' he said.

Peter looked at him pityingly. 'Tourists? Just how much have we found to be touristy about here?'

Beck had to admit he had a point. 'OK. So they're doing some kind of business. This is a town, Pete. Business happens . . .'

The men paused as they passed the end of the passage. It was dim and they didn't see the boys lurking further down. One of the men put his head close to the other's.

'If the pilot doesn't play ball, we'll shoot him. Simple.' he muttered.

The other man simply looked at him impassively. Then he nodded and turned sharply as they continued towards the hotel entrance.

'Whoa . . .' Beck murmured when they were safely out of earshot.

Peter poked his head round the corner again. 'They're calling a taxi!'

'Good.' Beck followed his friend out into the lobby again. He was just in time to see the pair climbing into the back of a cab. 'Let them go.'

'Let them go?' Peter looked at him as if he was mad.

'Yes, let them go!' Beck said firmly. 'Look . . .'

He had been here once before. A few months earlier, in Colombia, he'd had a run-in with the corrupt chief of police of Cartagena. Ramirez had been mixed up with the *narcotráficantes* – drug traffickers. Beck knew what it was like to mix with people who might shoot you. Your best strategy was to stay safely away.

He paused as it all came flooding back to him. Peter used the opportunity to start heading for the entrance.

'I want to know where they're going.' He watched as the cab pulled away with the two men inside it. 'Come on! We'll get a taxi too!'

'Wait, wait, wait!'

But Peter was already halfway across the lobby and Beck couldn't stop him. 'You . . .' He tried hard to think of a good reason that might persuade Peter to stay. 'You don't have any money!'

'No, but you do,' Peter said logically. 'Fifty quid, if I remember correctly.'

'But that wasn't for—' Beck began.

Peter was at the doors. Beck swore and ran after him towards the line of taxis waiting outside the hotel. He reached his friend just in time to see him signalling the next one.

The taxi pulled up and the driver leaned over. 'Where to, gentlemen?' he called.

Beck shuffled nervously. No, he didn't want to be involved . . . but he had a horrible feeling Peter would get involved anyway, and someone had to keep him out of trouble. 'We'll follow them, right? But that's all.'

And, he thought privately, it would be more interesting than another day in the pool . . .

'Sure.' Peter was already climbing into the back seat. Beck tumbled in after him and pulled the door shut as Peter pointed after the men's taxi and said, 'Follow that cab!'

The driver flashed a huge African smile back at them. 'I have waited all my life for someone to say that!'

He pressed the accelerator to the floor and the cab shot out into the traffic.

CHAPTER FIVE

'So where are you gentlemen from? London? That is fantastic! I have always wanted to visit London. Is this your first visit to Sierra Leone? Are you enjoying our lovely country?'

The taxi driver grinned broadly as he fired questions at Beck and Peter. More often than not he was looking at them too, which meant he was not looking at the road. Apparently he relied on telepathy to tell him what the traffic was doing. Either that or he was just steering a random course and everyone else was getting out of his way.

It seemed to be a gift of taxi drivers the world over, and it worked. Beck kept his eyes fixed firmly on the cab they were following.

'Now then' – the driver finally turned to look

where he was going – 'it seems your friends are heading for the airport. I can't think where else this road would take them. Will you be requiring a return trip?'

'Yes,' Beck said.

'Maybe not immediately,' said Peter. He looked challengingly at Beck.

Beck sighed. 'Maybe not immediately,' he agreed. At least, he thought with relief, there would be other Europeans around at the airport. He and Peter would have a far better chance of blending in. The men probably wouldn't recognize them and wouldn't dream that they had been followed.

Probably. Not that Beck intended to get so close to the men that they could be recognized anyway.

'Well, no sweat. I'll be in the taxi rank if you want a ride back to your hotel.' The driver chuckled. '"Follow that cab!" I actually had someone say "Follow that cab!" My wife will never believe— Oh.'

Suddenly he sounded surprised. Peter and Beck were immediately alert.

'What is it?'

'They have driven past the terminal. They're not

going to— Oh, I see. They are heading for the cargo area. Still want to follow?'

The boys looked at each other. Beck saw the fire in Peter's eyes.

'Yes,' he said, intrigued. 'Why not?'

The driver dropped them off by the airport fence, a hundred metres short of the service gate where the men had got out of their taxi. He gave them a final 'Good luck!' and drove off back to the terminal. Beck and Peter walked along the fence and peered into the cargo area on the other side of the gate. High wire mesh ran along the road separating them from the airport proper.

Over to one side was a large hangar. Its doors were wide open so they could see that it was big enough to contain several small planes, which stood scattered around inside. The two men were walking purposefully towards the hangar.

Parked in front was a plane that Beck didn't recognize. It had propellers, a boxy body and a short row of passenger windows down its side. Instinct made Beck count the engines: two of them. The aircraft looked worn and well used. There was a logo on the tail – an outline of a lion's head.

The service gate was padlocked but a small gap beneath the wire mesh allowed both boys to slide under it. Peter went first and Beck swiftly followed. No one noticed them slithering under the wire at the far end of the main airport perimeter. They were in. They looked around cautiously.

There was a small portakabin next to the hangar, about thirty metres from Beck and Peter. The words LION MOUNTAIN AIRCRAFT HIRE, with the same lion's-head logo, were marked in flaky paint above its windows. A man came out of the portakabin and greeted the pair from the hotel, shaking their hands and leading them back inside.

'Quick,' Peter said as he scuttled forward, camera in hand.

They crept up to the portakabin, taking care to stay out of sight of the windows. The windows were open and as they approached they could hear voices. One man – Beck guessed it was the one from the hire place – was chatty and friendly. The others – the men they had followed – answered in grunts and monosyllables.

'A few formalities with the paperwork, gentlemen. Please sign here . . . and here . . . Thank you . . . Now, here are copies of the hire insurance agreement, which you must read and sign . . .'

Beck craned his head round the corner of the portakabin. The plane stood just a few metres away. The wide sliding door in its side was open and he could see that the interior was packed with wooden crates. The men were hiring the plane and it was obviously fully loaded. How long before they took off?

Peter had seen the same thing; his thoughts had probably followed the same path. Beck saw the gleam in his eye. He gently pulled his friend back, round to the other side of the portakabin. There were no windows here and they could talk, as long as they kept their voices down.

'OK,' Beck murmured. 'If they're smuggling anything it's probably on board already. So we go back to the main airport building. We find a policeman – we tell him . . . something. Anything. Anything that will make him come and look. We've done our bit . . .'

But the gleam hadn't left Peter's eyes. 'Or *we* could take a look!' he urged, so eager he barely kept his voice down. He fiddled with his camera excitedly. 'Evidence! That will make the policeman take notice!'

'Are you *crazy*? They're right in there! They could come out at any moment—'

'They're filling in paperwork. That takes for ever. We peep in, open a crate, take a photo and get out again. It'll take seconds. Come on!'

And he was gone. Beck wanted to scream, but short of physically dragging Peter away – which would certainly make a noise, and get them spotted – he couldn't do anything about it. He glanced around nervously, paused, then followed.

CHAPTER SIX

Peter had the sense to scurry the long way round the portakabin, so no one inside would see him. He hopped up into the plane as if he belonged there and crouched by the nearest crate. His fingers scrabbled at the lid. 'Give me a hand!' he whispered.

Beck climbed up swiftly after his friend.

The inside of the plane had benches down either side. Opposite the door was a wire-framed locker with several brightly coloured jumpsuits hanging inside. Helmets and goggles lay on the floor of the locker – along with some parachutes looking like a pile of canvas rucksacks. This was a hire aircraft, Beck remembered. He guessed it was used by the local skydiving club – as well as anyone else who wanted to put money down.

At the front of the plane was the door leading into the empty cockpit. It was ajar and Beck could just make out the instrument panel.

The crates had been stacked in a row down the middle of the plane, two crates wide and two high. Peter reached for the nearest one; Beck went to the other side and they looked at each other, then prised off the lid.

Dull silver circles shone back at them, arranged in neat rows. The crate was full of tightly packed cans. Beck reached in and pulled one out.

'Fish,' he whispered, surprised. According to the label the tin contained tuna in spring water, but that didn't stop Peter raising his camera and taking a shot. 'What? Did you think the crates would be full of loose diamonds?'

'They could be *in* the tins,' Peter said stubbornly as he squinted into the lens. 'How can we open one?'

'Just stick it in your pocket and let's get out of—'

'Yes. All loaded and ready.'

It was a man's voice and it came from right outside the plane.

Peter froze. Beck glanced quickly out of the door.

There was a man there, partly in view, foot poised in mid step, head turned away. He hadn't seen either of them yet, and they had about three seconds before he did. Beck vaulted silently across the row of crates in one swift movement and pulled Peter down out of sight. They lay flat on the floor of the plane, hearts pounding and ears pricked for every sound.

Someone out of earshot must have asked the man a question. Beck shuddered. If he hadn't shouted like that, they would never have known he was there until it was too late.

'*I'll warm 'em up*,' the man called. '*We can take off in five.*'

And then there was the sound of the man climbing into the plane.

Beck peeped up above the crates. The man wore a leather pilot's jacket with the lion logo on the back. If he worked for Lion Mountain Aircraft Hire, Beck reckoned, maybe he wasn't a smuggler. He might not know who or what his passengers were. But that wouldn't necessarily make him any friendlier towards a pair of prying stowaway boys.

The pilot went forward to the cockpit and

dropped into the left-hand seat; a moment later the plane shook as the two engines roared into life.

Beck tugged at Peter's sleeve. 'Out,' he mouthed, though there was little chance of being heard over the engine's racket. Pale and sweating, Peter nodded. He fastened his camera back into its pouch and they both tentatively stood up –

– and then quickly dropped back down again. One of the men they had followed was approaching the aircraft. He climbed up behind the pilot, then sat down in the right-hand seat.

Beck gritted his teeth. That was two men. There was still a third – the other guy they had followed from the hotel. Was he going to come on the flight? Where was he? Would he see them getting off?

Well, they didn't have a choice. They had to get off *now*. They stood up and climbed quickly over the crates.

This time they made it as far as the door. They had a good view of the portakabin, and of the third man just leaving it. He paused to shut the door, then turned towards the plane.

There was no time to jump back across the

crates again. Beck yanked Peter to one side, out of sight of the door. The only place they could go now was the back of the plane. There was a small galley there, just where the plane started to narrow, with a toilet opposite. Beck pushed Peter down behind the galley, and just had time to shut himself into the even smaller toilet before the man climbed aboard.

Beck cracked the door open by the tiniest amount and peered out. He saw the man grab the handle of the door and slide it shut, then check that it was firmly closed; finally he went to join his friends, shutting the cockpit door behind him.

Peter and Beck exchanged glances. Peter was even paler and sweatier than before. He looked like he was about to be sick. Beck didn't feel much better. They were sealed in the plane and there was nothing they could do about it.

Then he clutched at the bulkhead, because the plane had lurched into motion. With its two unwilling passengers it lumbered and bounced across the airport tarmac. A brief pause, and then the engines bellowed twice as loud as before and it hurtled down the runway at full power.

CHAPTER SEVEN

Beck's thoughts raced as the plane started to climb. He didn't know how far it was going, or where, but it would take some minutes to reach cruising height. Chances were the three men would stay seated in the front – at least until the plane could level out.

So now would be his best chance to discuss things with Peter.

He crept out of the toilet and crouched down next to his friend.

'Sorry.' Peter had to say it quite loudly over the sound of the engines, but there was little chance of them being heard. The plane wasn't soundproofed like an airliner would have been. 'It's all my fault. We should have just gone to find a policeman.'

Beck studied his friend. Peter's eyes were wide

and the colour hadn't come back to his face yet. He was still very frightened. But his jaw was set and there was a determined twist to his mouth. He wasn't going to let the fear beat him. He was going to face up to what he had got them into.

A sudden flashback rushed into Beck's mind. It had been lurking on the edges of his memory ever since they got on board the plane, triggered by the sight of the parachutes. He remembered standing in the doorway of a plane very like this, with the ground 12,000 feet below. He was wearing a helmet, goggles and a jumpsuit, and the weight of a parachute tugged at his back. His hands were braced against the frame and the plane's slip-stream seemed to pluck at him with a thousand tiny fingers.

The instructor had put his face close to Beck's. 'Afraid?' he had called. Beck had nodded and the man grinned. 'You've got to have a little fear to be brave!' he shouted, and gave Beck the thumbs-up; then Beck had jumped.

Yes, Beck thought, you had to be afraid to be brave. If you weren't overcoming fear then it wasn't bravery, just stupidity. And that was what Peter had been doing.

And so, even though he could have spent the next half-hour telling Peter exactly what kind of idiot he was, he pushed the matter to one side. They had more pressing things on their minds.

'OK,' Beck said. 'Here's how it is. We're in trouble either way. If these guys really are just transporting tins of tuna then we're in less trouble than if . . . Well, you know.' *If they're smuggling diamonds . . .* was what he meant.

Peter nodded. 'You heard what they said about being willing to shoot the pilot.'

'Yeah . . .' Beck scratched his jaw. He didn't want to go there. 'Maybe it was just an expression . . .'

Peter didn't look convinced; Beck certainly didn't feel convinced. But under the circumstances, he had to know exactly where they stood.

'We don't even know where they're going . . .' he began.

'Morocco,' Peter said unexpectedly.

Beck blinked. 'How do you know that?'

Peter nodded at the nearest crate. 'Says so.'

Beck followed his gaze. Sure enough, stencilled in black paint along one side were some serial numbers and the words: EXPORTED UNDER LICENCE TO KINGDOM OF MOROCCO.

Beck bit his lip and tried to remember his African geography. You studied it on a map and it all looked so close together. You forgot Africa was vast. How far away was Morocco?

'OK,' he said uncertainly, 'that's probably . . . what? A good three-hour flight. At the end of that they're going to find us, if we don't tell them we're here.'

Peter stared at him as if he was mad. 'But if they're—'

'I know, I know. If they're smugglers . . .' Beck didn't finish the sentence; he bit his lip again, hard, thinking. 'Stay here. I'm going to see if I can hear what they're saying.'

Leaving Peter where he was before he could object, and more than a little afraid, Beck edged quickly down the line of crates towards the front of the aircraft.

He kept to the right-hand side of the plane. If

someone came out of the cockpit, hopefully the door would be between him and them. The plane was still climbing and it was an uphill walk. Just before he got to the cockpit the plane turned suddenly and Beck was thrown against the crates. He could see why normal airlines always made you stay seated during this part of the journey. But then the plane straightened out and continued to climb.

He had reached the cockpit bulkhead. The engines seemed quieter now that he was in front of them; their noise was carried away by the plane's passage. There was a grille in the door, an air vent, and Beck could just make out voices.

But it didn't help him. The pilot was conducting one half of a conversation with air traffic control, acknowledging directions and reporting his course and height. The other two were chatting quietly. One of them sounded like a local; the other had a South African accent – Beck guessed he was probably the white man he had seen earlier. But he couldn't make out what they were saying.

Beck groaned to himself. He needed facts. Some indication of whether they were smugglers or not.

Then he felt the plane shift beneath his feet. They were levelling out at last. Through the door he heard the pilot talking to his passengers.

'On time and on course, gentlemen. As promised.'

'Good. Keep it that way and you get to live,' the South African replied menacingly.

Then they all fell silent once more.

Beck leaned against the bulkhead, feeling very cold. Every bone in his body told him that these guys were bad news.

There was no doubt in his mind now. If they were prepared to kill the pilot, then why would they hesitate to kill *them*? He made his way quickly back down the plane towards Peter. The options raced through his mind. They were going to have to get off the plane without being discovered. If they didn't, then they would be killed.

The only question was, when?

CHAPTER EIGHT

Peter's eyes opened wide in disbelief. They had both squeezed into the plane's toilet, where Beck had given him the good news.

'Jump?' he squeaked. *'Jump?'*

But after the initial shock, Beck saw a change come over him. Peter summoned up his courage and calmed down. His voice grew steadier. Beck had told him what the men at the front of the plane had said. Peter drew the same conclusions and knew there was no point in arguing.

'OK,' he said simply. 'How?'

'Parachutes,' Beck said, jerking a thumb at the packs hanging in the locker.

'Well, yeah, but have you jumped before?'

'Yes . . .' Beck told him, before adding under his breath, 'Just the once.'

Peter looked at him. He was trusting him, Beck realized. Peter had known him for years: he didn't need to be told that Beck had survived in jungles and frozen mountains. He knew all that.

Beck felt like someone was flipping a switch inside his head. It sent him into survival mode. He knew what to do; with Peter's help, he could get them through this.

'We're going to wait as long as we can,' Beck told him. 'I don't know exactly how high we are but we're still flying a lot higher and a lot faster than normal skydiving altitude. If we're over about twelve thousand feet then we could pass out from lack of oxygen. But if we wait until we're near the end of the journey, the plane will be lower and slower.'

'And a lot further from where we started,' Peter pointed out.

Beck pulled a knowing face. 'Yes. But if my geography is right then we'll be flying over the Sahara at the moment. It's one of the hottest and driest places on earth. If we land in the middle of that, then it'll kill us almost as quickly as those guys at the front.'

'You've been in deserts before, though.'

'Yeah, but I had a bit more time to prepare. I can do it, only . . .' He trailed off and looked sideways at his friend. The right words jumbled together inside him and wouldn't come out in the right order. What he wanted to say was something like: *I can't take a passenger. If you're expecting* me *to do everything then we're dead before we even begin.*

'I've always had help too.' He sounded awkward even to his own ears. 'There's always been an adult to help me get stuff done.'

'OK,' Peter said simply. 'What can I do?'

Beck grinned with relief. Peter understood.

'Right. First, search the galley. Go through it and pick out anything – anything at all – that could be useful to us down there.'

'I'm on it!'

While Peter did that, Beck turned his attention to the parachute locker. It was padlocked shut but the padlock wasn't strong. Beck jimmied it open with a screwdriver from a tool kit in the galley. He pulled out the first two parachutes and put them down by the sliding door of the plane.

Then he returned to the locker to see what else he could find. The mass of jumpsuits smelled stale as he rummaged among them. Apparently they weren't washed after being used. They were also all adult size – too big for him or Peter. But he could take some goggles and helmets.

Beck was about to close the locker again when his eye caught one more thing. 'Aha!' He pulled out a musty canvas rucksack and tipped it out. It held a skydiving logbook and a half-full packet of cigarettes but nothing more. Beck put it with the rest of the equipment.

'How are you doing, Pete?' he asked.

'OK . . . I think . . .'

Peter laid out his own haul. 'There's not much food in the galley, but there is this . . .' He held up a small carton. 'Aircraft survival pack. It's got some rations and—'

'Yeah, we'll take that.'

Next was a white metal box marked with a red cross.

'Medical kit . . .'

'Yup.'

'Oh, and one of these . . .' Peter held up a penknife. 'All the other cutlery's plastic so I didn't think it would be very helpful.'

'Perfect!' Beck checked it – a single blade folding back into a wooden handle. The edge wasn't as sharp as it could be but it still had a nice point on it. 'Yup, that's good.'

'There's, um, these . . .' Peter showed Beck a pair of large, clear plastic bottles full of fizzy drink. Beck pulled a face when he saw what was in them. It was the local brand of cola – a carbonated chemical brew designed to make you even thirstier and buy more.

'We could use the bottles,' he said. 'We'll tip them out and fill them up from the tap.'

'And that's about it . . .'

'Good work, Peter.' Beck saw a small flush of pride creep over his friend's face.

He remembered the tool kit where he had found

the screwdriver. He went back for another look through. There wasn't much there he could use except for a torch, which he pocketed.

'Um, dunno if this would be any good . . .' Peter was pointing at something that hung next to the door.

Beck rolled his eyes. 'Duh! Of course.'

It was an emergency axe, the kind used to cut your way out of the hull if the plane crashed. Beck pulled it from its housing. He didn't know how far they would have to walk once they had jumped. The axe was heavy, and as they grew more and more tired it would feel heavier, but it might still be useful.

'Right,' he said. 'Help me get this lot into the rucksack and then we'll get you fitted for your first parachute jump!'

CHAPTER NINE

'Oof.' Peter staggered a little when the weight of the parachute dropped onto his shoulders.

'Just shrug it on like it's a rucksack,' Beck told him.

Peter wiggled his shoulders and Beck loosely did up the chest strap.

'Right,' he said, turning to the leg straps. 'This is the important bit . . .'

The leg straps were a pair of loops hanging down from the bottom of the parachute. With a bit of help, Peter worked a leg through each of them, then stood while Beck tightened them around his thighs and checked them for twists. Then he adjusted the chest strap and tightened it all up. He had to pull the straps in almost as far as they would go to fit Peter's small frame.

'Why so important?' Peter asked.

Beck grinned up at him. 'These are what hold you up. Without these you'd just drop straight out of the harness when the chute opens.'

'So,' Peter said faintly, 'when it opens you're dangling by your—'

'Exactly.'

'Eek.'

Beck finished by tugging on the shoulder straps to make sure that the parachute lay flat and snug against Peter's back.

'Right,' he said. He looked into Peter's eyes. 'I don't know how high we are and we don't want to be in freefall for long. It takes many jumps to master keeping your body stable in a hundred and thirty mile-per-hour freefall. This is a crash course, not a freefall display. So, we're going to hop and pop. That means we jump together and I will pull your cord for you as we leave the plane, right?' He patted the emergency release – a handle on a much thicker strap against Peter's ribs on his left side. 'And I'll pull mine right after that.'

'Now, once your chute's open' – Beck clenched

his fists and held them above his shoulders – 'there'll be a pair of toggles up here, right? One on either side. And you can use them to steer your chute. It's called a ram-air chute. It opens up like a wing. Pull left to go left, right to go right and, just before you land, pull them both down together firmly. That will make the chute tilt upwards, which means you slow down, so you should touch down nice and gentle. Got that?'

'Toggles, left, right, both down together, nice and gentle.' Peter's voice was wavering. 'People do this every day, right?'

'Every day,' Beck assured him. He picked up the goggles and helmets, handing one set to Peter, then stepped back for a final look at his handiwork. Peter's eyes darted around nervously. The chute looked as natural on him as scuba gear on a cat, but it would work.

'Anything else . . . anything else . . .' Beck thought out loud.

'Um,' Peter said, 'I know where we could get some extra food.'

Beck's face lit up. 'Yeah? Where?'

Peter simply nodded back down the cabin. Beck

threw a puzzled glance at the cockpit. What did his friend mean? Steal the pilot's sandwiches?

And then it struck him. 'Duh!' he said again, and scowled at Peter's broad grin. 'Right.'

Together they lifted the lid off the crate again and filled up the remaining space in the rucksack with tins of tuna.

'And there's a can opener in the galley,' Peter said before Beck could ask. 'I remember it.'

'Right.' Beck quickly retrieved it and slipped it into the rucksack, then tied it firmly closed. 'My turn.'

'You can't really wear a chute and that . . .'

'I'll wear the rucksack strapped to my leg. Chute first.'

'We've still got some time to go, haven't we?' Peter asked nervously as Beck picked up the other chute.

'Sure,' Beck grunted. He heaved the pack up onto his shoulders. 'But if we get ready now, we can jump at a moment's notice. They'll be on to us as soon as we open the door so we'll have to be quick about it. Here, give me a hand with—'

At exactly that moment there was a sharp bark from the cockpit.

'Who the hell are you?'

It was the South African. They all locked eyes for a moment and then three things happened simultaneously:

The man's hand flashed inside his coat.

Beck frantically lifted a leg into the first leg strap, hopping and almost falling over as he did so.

And there was a bellow of pain from the front of the plane.

One of Beck's legs was in. He spared a moment to look up in surprise as he tightened the buckle. The man was staggering back with his hand clamped to his face. Blood was pouring from his nose. Peter stood, poised, with a second can of fish in his hand.

Beck quickly turned his attention to his other leg strap.

'Why, you little . . .' The man's voice was choked with pain. He pawed again at his coat. This time Beck distinctly saw the handgrip of a pistol in its shoulder holster.

Peter threw again, hard, with unerring accuracy. He scored another direct hit on the man's head.

Beck vowed that he would never again call cricket a wuss's game. Peter was the main strike bowler for the under-fifteens XI and he was saving their lives.

'Hurry, Beck!' Peter called.

'I'm trying . . .'

The leg strap was a bit too tight and Beck couldn't get his leg into it. He was hopping around again as he tried to loosen it.

'What the hell is happening?'

The second man had appeared. He immediately took in the situation and ducked down behind the crates before Peter could throw anything at him. He also pulled his friend down.

'Give it up, boys!' he called. 'You've nowhere to go! We won't hurt you . . .'

It would have been more convincing if the other man hadn't poked his head, and his gun, up above the protection of the crates. This time Peter's flung can caught his gun hand. The man swore as he pulled his hand back.

Another rain of tin cans. The men could have just braved it and shot them, but they probably didn't want to open up with guns inside an aeroplane. But any moment now they would decide to charge and simply overrun the boys.

'There's no time!' Beck shouted. His chute was only half on, but he didn't have any choice. It was go now or die. He lunged for the handle of the door and heaved.

The door slid open and it felt like a hurricane filling the interior of the plane. Peter staggered back and bumped into Beck.

Both men stood up, struggling for balance, and raised their guns.

Beck only had time to slip one arm through the rucksack's straps and grab Peter around the waist; then he pushed Peter backwards out of the plane. They were gone.

CHAPTER TEN

Air and ground and sky whirled around them as they tumbled uncontrollably. A mighty wind roared in their ears and Beck was almost blinded. He hadn't had time to pull down his goggles. Whenever he opened his eyes, the blast of wind simultaneously filled them with tears and dried them up.

Peter's yell rang in his ears. It went on and on and on. Beck still had his arms wrapped around him, and the rucksack was bulky between them. The boys were locked tightly together and plummeting straight down. Beck was the heavier, with the rucksack, so he was falling first.

Still keeping one arm around Peter's waist, Beck fumbled for his friend's ripcord and felt his fingers close around it. He yanked, hard, at the same time pushing Peter away from him. A whipping, cracking noise. Then a blur of colour and motion right in front of Beck's face. Suddenly Peter was whipped up out of sight.

Now Beck had to get himself stable. He arched his back and flung his arms out wide; the wind flipped him over so that he was facing down towards the earth. Now he was in a stable position and, despite everything, he grinned. This was more like it. He didn't feel like he was falling. The pressure of the wind against him made him feel as if he was just lying in bed, being blasted by hot air. If he didn't have one arm still through the rucksack straps, he could have started doing somersaults, or banking from side to side, putting on all kinds of aerobatics.

'You can do anything a bird can do,' his instructor had told them on the course. Then he had added, with a wry grin, 'Except go back up.'

And that was the point. Beck was falling towards the Earth at about 130 m.p.h. This was no time for games. He felt for his own ripcord and pulled.

The same whip-crack in his ears, and then a force seized his whole body and yanked him upwards. The furious rush of wind in his ears died down to a gentle rumble. The chute was fully open above him, a tent that blocked out the sky. Air pressure filled it out into a thick wing that thrummed like a sail. He was suspended in mid-air above Africa, and despite everything he gave a whoop of triumph.

He looked up and saw Peter's chute, already far above him. It was a red and white rectangle, sixty square metres of silk, soaring in the sky.

They had survived. So far. Beck was still clutching the rucksack in his arms, so he wedged it between his knees and reached up for his control toggles. He steered himself in a wide, gentle circle. He would pull both brakes gently to slow himself down until Peter reached the same height, so that they could land together.

The Sahara wheeled beneath him. It was a wind-sculpted landscape of sand, rocky canyons and plateaus. It made a vast wrinkled patchwork, with shades of brown stretching from horizon to horizon. A quarter of it was dunes. The rest was sun-baked rock, dry earth or salt pans.

Beck looked vainly for any kind of landmark that

could tell him where they were. No sign of any sea or rivers. Some of those darker lines would be dried-up riverbeds but they told him nothing. There might have been some mountains on the horizon – but they were so far away it was impossible to tell through the haze. Not a single road, no sign of any town or village or . . . anything. His exhilaration died away as the magnitude of where they were fully dawned on him.

Six months earlier he had led his friends through the Colombian rainforest. They had had days to prepare, stocking up on supplies and then living off the land as they went.

A couple of months ago, with another friend, he had traversed frozen mountains in the depths of Alaska. But they had had proper clothing for the expedition, a few basic supplies, and they had picked up more food as they went. And in a land of snow and ice it hadn't been hard to find water.

The Sahara Desert had very little food and even less water. They were wearing what they had put on when they got up that morning. And he was about to land in the middle of nowhere with nothing but a few emergency bits and pieces thrown together in a rucksack.

'Beck!'

Peter was now dangling in the air at the same height as him but about fifty metres away. Beck pulled on a toggle and his chute banked towards his friend's. He was careful not to get too close. A mid-air collision would tangle their chutes and kill them both. Beck positioned himself so that he was flying parallel to Peter with a good twenty metres between their canopies.

'How are you feeling?' Beck called back.

'Bloody terrified! And my glasses fell off!'

Beck grinned. That was the least of their problems. He could see that Peter had managed to put his goggles on.

'Try steering. Pull the left toggle,' Beck shouted across.

'Whoa!'

Peter banked sharply away from him to his left and almost turned a full circle. He also dropped down below Beck.

'Not so hard. OK. Come right. More gently . . .'

Peter turned right again with a bit more control. Now his canopy was below Beck's feet. Beck carefully steered himself away. His instructor had warned about what happened when two chutes got on top of each other. The lower one would steal the upper one's air and the top one would collapse. Probably on top of the bottom one.

OK, he thought, *now what? We land and . . . um . . .*

On the ground, they were going to have to decide where to head. He looked at his watch. They had been in the plane for over an hour in total, gathering their supplies and getting ready. That meant they were probably more than halfway to Morocco. It made sense to keep heading north.

He looked up at the plane, now dwindling into a dot in the distance. It was still maintaining its course towards Morocco – that was the way they wanted to go too, so it made sense to head in that direction.

'Follow me,' Beck shouted.

He pulled on the control toggles, steering towards the dot in the sky. 'We're going this way.'

It took about five more minutes for them to touch

down. Beck didn't know how much distance they had covered but at least they'd been travelling in the right direction. As they got lower he could feel the heat beating back at him.

It was strange how you didn't actually notice things on the ground getting bigger until the last moment, when they suddenly rushed up at you. A dune reared up beneath Beck's feet. In a moment it had swelled up until it filled his vision completely. He hauled down on both toggles. This made the chute tilt up a little, which slowed him down as he prepared for the impact. He grabbed the rucksack and broke into a run the moment his feet touched the ground. A paratrooper couldn't have done it better, he thought. He was down.

He looked around. The landscape was dry and desolate. Baked earth, rocks and sand that would be almost too hot to touch. Beck had heard that a definition of a desert was somewhere that got less than twenty-five centimetres of rain a year. This certainly looked like it matched that description.

'Ah-h-h-h . . .'

Peter shot overhead and disappeared the other

side of the dune. Beck had told him how to slow down but he wasn't sure Peter had remembered. Knowing you are about to hit the ground can make you forget all your training – Beck knew that only too well from his own experience.

He pulled on one of the steering lines, which collapsed his chute so that it wouldn't pull him along the ground. Then he remembered that he hadn't told Peter about that little trick and he swore to himself. He released his harness and hurried over the dune, feeling the hot sand shift and squirm beneath his feet.

Peter was on the ground; his canopy was still billowing up behind him like a giant brightly striped animal. He struggled to his feet but it pulled him over onto his front and dragged him along the ground. Beck hurried after him. Peter kept trying to regain his feet but he was continually tugged forward.

The canopy made straight for a row of scrubby bushes in the shade of a rock. The spiky branches snagged the silk, though the chute still billowed as it struggled to get free.

Peter lay on the ground, still a little dazed, and

fumbled at the buckles of his harness. The straps fell away as Beck came up to him and held out a hand, finally pulling him free of his chute.

As Beck helped his friend to his feet, he saw that his eyes were a little glazed and he was already sweating in the heat. The sun pressed down and the wind felt as if someone was holding a giant hairdryer in front of them. Beck could feel the heat of the sand through the soles of his trainers.

He assessed the situation: they could well be the only humans for hundreds of miles around. If he didn't use every ounce of his skill, he knew that dehydration and sunburn could kill them just as easily as a smuggler's bullet. It would just take a little longer.

During the day temperatures could soar to fifty-five degrees Centigrade. A human's core body temperature only had to rise 3.5 degrees for heatstroke to set in – which led swiftly to cramps, exhaustion and, ultimately, death.

During the night you could just as easily get hypothermia as the temperature plummeted under the clear night skies.

This was the impossible world of the desert.

Beck grinned at his friend, baring his teeth without any humour.

'Welcome to the Sahara!'

CHAPTER ELEVEN

'We need to get out of the sun,' Beck said firmly.

Peter gazed around, squinting in the glare. There was nothing but sand and scrubby vegetation as far as the eye could see: small clusters of tough grass or bushes. Nearby was a leafless, thorny tree about the same height as a grown man.

'Yeah, I think I saw a nice house over there,' he said.

'We brought our shelter with us.' Beck put the rucksack he was holding down on the ground. He felt about in it for the penknife, then headed over to the snagged parachute. 'Hold the canopy for me, will you . . .'

Peter held the silk taut and Beck used the knife to slice two long ribbons from the upper layer of the canopy. They were about two metres long and half a metre wide. It wasn't a clean cut. The 'silk' was actually nylon that frayed along the edges where Beck sliced it, and the blade was blunt. But it would do.

'Wrap it around your head like a headscarf.'

He passed one of the pieces to Peter and demonstrated with the other. His own piece went around his head twice and covered his face so that just his eyes showed. He tucked the loose ends into the neck of his shirt. 'You need to protect your head as much as possible – if your brain fries, you're dead. And try to breathe through your nose, not your mouth. Breathing through your mouth just dries up moisture.'

'Right.' Peter wrapped his piece of silk round his own head, with a bit of help from Beck. When he finished, his eyes peeped through the narrow gap that he had left. 'What next?'

'Over here,' Beck said. He took the axe and went over to the thorn tree he had seen earlier.

The tree's branches stuck out in different directions as if imitating a mad conductor, arms going everywhere at once. Beck selected a pair of leafless branches that were about a metre and a half long and not much thicker than his own arm. From each length he cut or scraped away the side branches and twigs, then swung the axe at the point where they met the trunk. It took five minutes to cut both branches completely free and they tumbled to the sand, one after the other.

Next, Peter held the branches upright while Beck used the flat of the axe blade to hammer them into the ground, about two metres apart. The boys were left with two crooked poles standing about shoulder height. One was a little taller than the other.

Beck turned his attention back to the parachute canopy. 'And now hold the silk steady again . . .' The chute consisted of two layers, the upper and the lower surfaces; between these were empty cells of silk. They filled with air as the parachute moved, giving it its shape. There was plenty of silk for Beck's purposes.

The section that Beck cut off was about five metres long and three wide. He then used the knife to cut a pair of holes in the long edge and used parachute lines to tie it to the two poles, about ten centimetres from the top. The cord was made of tough, interwoven strands of nylon. It stretched, it was flexible, and Beck could think of about a thousand different uses for it. Now the layer of silk dangled between the two poles with a flap of silk hanging down at either end.

Beck cut a pair of shorter bits of wood to act as tent pegs, and used them to stake the other long edge of the silk down to the ground. Out of nowhere, they now had a small, wedge-shaped tent. 'The entrance faces north, away from the sun,' Beck added.

'Hey, I'm in!' Peter said eagerly, but Beck pulled him back.

'Not quite, you're not. Give me a hand again . . .'

They went back to the canopy and Beck started cutting away another piece of silk.

'Look, the sun's shining right through it,' he said, nodding at the tent. The silk was thin and light, and it was almost glowing with the light of the sun behind it. 'It won't be much shelter. But now . . .'

They took the new piece of silk over to the shelter and went through the same process. This time Beck tied it nearer the top of the poles, while Peter again staked down the edges. Now the tent had two layers, about ten centimetres apart. Both ends of the shelter could be folded open, which allowed the breeze through, and the interior was shaded.

'And *now*,' Beck said, 'sir may retire to his room.'

Peter went in cautiously, ducking his head and brushing away a few twigs and stones from where he wanted to lie. Then he stretched himself out on the sand and breathed out loudly.

Beck lay down next to him and propped himself up on one elbow. He glanced at the silk. It was still faintly translucent, but inside it was nowhere near as bright as it had been. The second layer made all the difference. In fact it made more of a difference than Peter probably realized.

'This is how the Bedouin make their tents,' Beck explained. 'With two layers, air can pass between them and that carries the heat away.'

'Still hot. You could boil a cup of water out there.'

'Yeah, but it's not as hot as it could be.' Beck nodded at the bright sunlight, just a metre or so

away from the shade of the tent. 'Out there it's about
. . . oh, a hundred and twenty.'

'*What?* That's more than boiling!'

'Fahrenheit.'

'Oh. What's that in real temperature?'

Beck thought for a moment. 'Uh . . . roughly fifty
degrees. So it's only halfway to boiling. But in here,
in the shade, it'll be way cooler.'

'Neat trick,' Peter commented after a moment.
'The tent. The Bedouin thing.'

'Well, they've lived in the desert for thousands of
years, so they know a bit about it. Did you ever
wonder why desert people wear long flowing
clothes?'

'Because they haven't invented T-shirts?' Peter's
deadpan voice made it quite clear he didn't really
think that.

Beck grinned and shook his head. 'Same principle as the tent. Layers of air between the robes help
cool them down, and they need to cover up to keep
the sun off them. Maybe we can't quite match that
but we can still protect our bare skin. The wind
blows like a hairdryer. You sweat and it dries you up

before you even notice. So you sweat some more, and it dries you up again, and in no time you're completely dehydrated. *Plus* you get a lovely dose of sunburn into the bargain. So we need to keep the sun off us during the day and we need to wrap up warm at night.'

Peter propped himself up, looked at Beck and then at himself. At least he was wearing long, loose trousers and a long-sleeved shirt. He was protected against sunburn. Beck was in a T-shirt and long shorts that stopped halfway between his knees and his ankles. Good for lounging beside the hotel pool. Not great for surviving in a desert.

'So where do we get . . . ?' Then Peter mentally answered his own question. 'Duh. Of course.'

He nodded upwards. They had two parachutes with them – all the extra material they could possibly need. Then he looked thoughtful. 'And what else do we need to do? Better tell me everything now.' He sat cross-legged, attentive and waiting.

CHAPTER TWELVE

Beck pushed himself up and sat facing Peter. His thoughts went back to what he had worked out coming down on the parachute. 'We're more than halfway to Morocco, so we're going to head north. I've no idea – and I mean, *no* idea – where we are – what country we're in—'

'Probably northern Mauritania or western Algeria,' Peter said unexpectedly. Beck looked impressed. 'So I got high marks in my geography project on northern Africa,' his friend explained.

'OK. But wherever we are, if we head north then we should reach Morocco . . . eventually. If we can stay alive that long.'

'Sure. Makes sense.' Peter traced circles idly in the sand with his finger. 'I also know that if we're walking to Morocco from the south then we will eventually meet the Atlas Mountains. That's our best chance of finding people.'

Beck remembered the mountains he had seen in the far distance, after his chute opened. He hoped they were the start of the Atlas Range. 'But for now we need to wait for the sun to die down.'

'OK.' Peter seemed to accept this. Beck realized he was showing the same calm trust he had shown back in the plane. Peter didn't know anything about survival, and Beck knew loads, so Peter was calmly putting himself in his hands. Beck hoped that if he ever had to rely on Peter for something that his friend was good at – photography? geography? – then he would be just as trusting in return.

'And as much as we can,' he went on, 'we're going to rest by day and travel by night. I have to warn you, the desert can get pretty cold at night, but we'll keep moving. If we have to, then we can wrap ourselves up in parachute silk. It won't be comfortable but it'll be a lot more comfortable than frying our brains out during the day.'

'Oh, and, er, Beck . . .' Peter was back to drawing

circles in the sand. It was obviously his signal for an awkward subject that he didn't want to bring up. Then he lifted his head and looked Beck in the eye. 'What do we do about food and water?'

'We get hungry and thirsty,' Beck said simply. Peter looked so surprised that he couldn't help laughing. 'Not completely. But we're going to be on very limited rations. If you eat just a little at frequent intervals, that's as good as having a proper meal every few hours. And if you eat too much you just use up water. Anyway, a guy can go weeks without food . . . but only about twenty-four hours out here without water.'

'And we need how many litres of water per day?' Peter asked.

'Four if we are resting in the shade. Thirteen if we're moving,' Beck said shortly. 'That's a lot of water—'

Peter interrupted: 'Well, we have a couple of bottles, and whatever's in those cans we brought. So you can see why I'm interested.'

'There's water in the desert,' Beck said. 'Even here. Look. There are plants growing.'

He gestured out of the shelter and Peter leaned forward to peer out.

'OK,' he said. He sounded surprised. 'So there's water. A little.'

'A little,' Beck agreed. 'We're going to get thirsty but, if we're smart, we're not going to die of it.'

'Suits me. Which way's north?'

Beck was pleased to get off the subject of water. Peter was absolutely right in everything he had said. There was water, and he did know how to find it. But there was precious little to be found. It was easy to waste time looking for it and just make yourself thirstier than before.

'Here, Peter, if you're travelling during the day, you can use your watch to navigate by. Look – hold it horizontal . . .'

'OK.' Peter levelled his wrist in front of his eyes.

Beck continued to explain how to find north using the hour hand and the sun.

Peter was impressed. 'Cool.' He studied his watch, thought for a moment and then twisted round again. He pointed straight out of the shelter. 'That's north.'

'Excellent.' Beck was smiling. Then he noticed . . .

'Pete, you've got a digital watch!' he exclaimed.

Peter looked innocently at him. 'Well, yeah, but if I know the time then I know where the hands would be if it had them, don't I? I just imagine a clock face with an hour hand and point the imaginary hand at the sun.'

Beck looked at him silently, and Peter grinned, and then they both dissolved into laughs.

'You know, I'd never thought of that.'

'I wish we had a GPS . . .' Peter said wistfully.

'Hmm.' Beck thought back to his previous two encounters with a GPS. 'The last time I used one of those the batteries ran down. And the time before that I accidentally dropped it into the sea.' He changed the subject. 'How hungry are you?' he asked Peter.

His friend looked thoughtful. 'Um. Not really. I had a huge breakfast.'

'OK. We're going to try and rest for the remainder of the day, then we'll eat something before we set off tonight.'

'You're the boss,' Peter said complacently, and he lay back on the sand with his hands behind his head. After a while his eyes closed. The wind blowing past ruffled the silk with a soothing sound. The sand inside had cooled down and the air was nicely warm. The shelter was pleasant to be in. It was possibly the only pleasant two square metres in the entire desert, but it was theirs.

Beck lay down too. His thoughts were still full of what lay ahead and it took him much longer to drop off.

He had been putting on as positive a face as possible for Peter's benefit. He had survived the Kalahari Desert and the Australian Outback. He could do so here too. But those other expeditions had been undertaken with plenty of planning, and with experts to help him. Here there was no planning at all, and *he* was the expert.

They could head north. That bit wasn't hard. But Beck knew he could be leading them both into a furnace from which they would never escape.

CHAPTER THIRTEEN

Getting sleep was easier said than done. Both of them snoozed for a little but that was all. The sun crept down as if it was reluctant to give up the chance to fry them. The shadow of the shelter slowly moved round.

Peter hugged his knees and gazed gloomily out at the desert. He seemed lost in a little world of his own. Beck didn't know what thoughts were running through his head but he couldn't afford to let his spirits sink.

'OK,' he said suddenly. Peter jumped. 'To work!'

There were preparations to make. Beck had already studied himself and Peter critically. They had to protect their bare skin – their arms, their legs, and above all their heads. Clothing was the most basic form of shelter in the desert. Ideally they should both be dressed like Peter, in shirt and trousers, both loose and long. During the day the clothes would let the air circulate around their bodies but keep their sweat from evaporating. During the night they would just help keep them warm.

But Beck wasn't wearing clothes like that and there was no point wishing he was. So with Peter's help he cut off another layer of parachute silk and a few more lengths of cord. This time he sliced the silk into squares about half a metre long. Then he poked holes along opposite edges and threaded more cord through. Finally he wrapped each square around one leg and used the cord to tie it just above the knee and then above the ankle. Now he had a silk legging that hung down to the ground.

'Armani eat your heart out,' Peter commented when he saw it.

Beck grinned. 'Now we'll make a couple of upper-body wraps for the both of us. They'll be extra protection from the wind and they'll keep us warm tonight—'

'Eek!'

Peter suddenly convulsed, scrambling to his feet before he remembered he couldn't stand up in the shelter. As it was he almost ended up in Beck's lap.

'What the—-?' Beck began.

'Spider! Big one!'

Beck peered past his friend.

The spider was about five centimetres across, with long, arched, hairy legs. It had stopped a little way inside the tent. The legs were yellow, like the sand, but the body was darker and bloated. In place of teeth it had a pair of large pincers.

'It – it just came scuttling in . . .' Peter stammered.

Beck looked at it thoughtfully. He reached carefully for the knife, and pounced. The spider twitched as he pinned it through its head, the pressure pushing it down into the sand. Beck used the blade to flick the head away, back in the direction it had come from. He picked the body up by one of its legs.

'It's a camel spider,' he told Peter. 'Not really poisonous – though it could give you a seriously nasty bite. They can shift along at up to ten miles per hour . . . but usually they just make for shade. It just wanted to get out of the sun. Handy to remember that you're not the only one who appreciates shade. In fact a snake without shade will die within a few hours. If you ever find a shady nook, or lift up a rock or anything, just be careful in case there's something else there first.'

'I'll remember,' Peter vowed.

'You know, in the desert, if something's poisonous it's *really* poisonous. There's so little food that it can't take the chance of its prey getting away. It wants to know that just one scratch will bring it down.'

'We've got stinging nettles at the bottom of our garden,' Peter said conversationally. 'That's about as poisonous as home gets—' He broke off and turned pale as Beck offered him the decapitated spider.

'Fancy a bite?'

'N-not really, no.'

''Kay.' Beck didn't want to do this but he had to make the point. He popped the spider's body into his mouth and crunched. There was a warm fluid explosion on his tongue. The innards were gooey and oozed between his teeth, as if he had just

96

swallowed a gobbet of snot and was swilling it back and forth. It tasted even worse. He had to press his lips together to stop the spider's guts oozing out. The legs were like twigs scraping against his tongue. When he swallowed, he could feel them all the way down his throat.

But he was now slightly better fed than he had been thirty seconds before. He turned to Peter and spoke earnestly.

'What I just said about the shade is the second lesson you need to learn. The first is that we're in this to survive. We only get one stab at being alive, because once you're dead you're dead for ever. In order to live we must both step outside our comfort zones. In fact, not just step. We must take a long running jump so that we land a long, long way away from normal existence and don't ever look back. We do whatever – and I mean *whatever* – it takes to survive. Got that?'

Peter bit his lip. 'Got it,' he said quietly.

'You're a good buddy, Peter – I mean, my best buddy. We'll get through this together, OK?'

'You bet, Beck. Thank you.'

A flash of movement caught Beck's eye. A sand beetle was picking its way towards the shade of the shelter. It was about three centimetres long, black fading to dusty grey. Like all beetles, it seemed to be slightly lost. It didn't really know where it was going – just that it was going somewhere.

Beck picked it up between two fingers and held it out to Peter, eyebrows raised.

His friend looked at it without enthusiasm. 'This will be a test to show I can do it, right?'

He held out his cupped hands. Beck dropped the beetle into them. Peter looked at the insect unhappily, then closed his eyes and crammed it into his mouth.

'Oh my god that is the most disgusting thing ever,' he mumbled. He screwed up his face thoughtfully. 'Mostly sand. A bit of old sock. Bits of . . . something. Salty.'

'Salty? Excellent. We'll be losing salt every time we sweat, which will be a lot. We'll make sure we eat plenty of these.'

Peter swallowed the beetle down. 'Can't wait . . .'

'Me neither. Let's get back to work.'

Once they got the hang of it, it didn't take long to finish their silk wraps. Beck stretched, then peered out of the shelter. The sun was now almost level with the sand dunes. The sky was lighting up in an orange flare that stretched across the horizon.

'Wow,' Peter breathed.

'Yeah,' Beck said again. He looked almost fondly at the sun. Earlier it had been a scorching presence so bright you couldn't look at it, and it would be again. But now it was a glowing orange ball that seemed suddenly much safer, and it lent itself to beautiful scenes like this.

'You sure get excellent sunsets in the desert,' Peter commented.

'It's the dust in the air. It scatters the light so that only the red wavelength gets through.' Beck glanced sidelong at his friend and shrugged. 'My dad used to tell me that as a kid,' he added quietly. Then, straight away, he added, 'It's time to go. Help me get the shelter down?'

It was a very convenient kind of tent, Beck

thought. It folded into two pieces of silk that either of them could carry without noticing it. He looked wistfully at the two parachutes. He was sure there were so many things he could use them for . . . but they were heavy. There was just too much silk. He contented himself with cutting off as much parachute cord as they could carry, and the complete upper layer of one of the parachutes. Then he looked thoughtfully at the ripcord that you pulled to open the chute in the first place – a metal handle tied to wire. The wire was made of several strands wound together. Wire could be good for snares. So he cut away the wire from its housing and folded it up with the parachute cord. The parachute container itself could be used as a kind of rucksack if they tied it up.

The last thing Beck did was get Peter to help him spread the remaining parachute silk out on the sand. 'Pin it down with rocks,' he told his friend. 'I don't want the wind blowing it away. If any plane flies over they might spot this and know someone is lost out here.'

Beck then laid some extra rocks out in the shape

of an arrow. 'This will tell anyone who spots it which way we have gone. OK, let's get moving.'

And the two boys set off on the journey of their lives.

CHAPTER FOURTEEN

The sun was below the level of the dune now and they were in the shade, though with plenty of light to see. After an hour of steady walking they broke open the emergency rations they had taken from the plane. It was a pack of six food bars – dried oats and fruit, compacted together.

'We'll eat one each now, another at midnight, and have the last for breakfast,' Beck decided. 'After that we're on cans of tuna and desert food.'

As they sat in the twilight, Peter looked mournfully at the bars. 'That full breakfast was a long time ago,' he commented.

'One now, and another at midnight,' Beck repeated.

'You da boss.'

They ate their bars and put on their packs again. Peter carried the parachute rucksack; Beck had the one with their supplies.

'Peter, can you set your watch to go off every . . . oh, thirty minutes?' Beck asked as they started off once more.

'Sure.' Peter's watch beeped as he set it. 'Why?'

'There's a tribe in Mexico,' Beck explained, 'called the Tarahumara. They live in the Chihuahua Desert . . .'

Peter sniggered. 'The Chihuahua Desert? Is that right next to the Pekinese Plains and the Small Yappy Mountains?'

'I know – it always makes me laugh too,' Beck said with a grin that Peter couldn't see behind his face wrappings. 'The Tarahumara conserve water by taking a mouthful and holding it there. They breathe through their noses. The water soaks slowly into their bodies and the mouthful lasts a lot longer than if they just swallowed it down. We're going to try it. It's difficult, and you really, really want to swallow, but you should be able to hold it for around fifteen minutes.'

He matched actions to words by taking a gulp

and carefully holding it in his mouth. Every part of him wanted to chug the whole bottle down. He saw the reluctance in Peter to stop drinking – the way he paused before taking the bottle away from his mouth and handing it back.

Beck looked at his friend, then glanced down at himself. They must make a strange sight in their silk ponchos and turbans, and him with his silk leggings too. But they were dressed as sensibly as they could be.

He nodded towards the north, towards Morocco, with a gesture that said, *Shall we?*

* * *

The faint glow of dusk lingered in the west for a while, but it soon faded away. The colours of the desert leached away into shades of grey. Peter saw Beck's outline grow dimmer until his friend looked like a solid ghost, trudging across the endless dunes.

'Walk so you're making good, heavy steps,' Beck told him. 'It'll scare off any snakes.'

Peter said nothing but his footsteps grew distinctly louder.

With the sun went the warmth of the day. Beck felt the skin on his arms goose-pimple, even beneath the silk. At least the poncho was keeping a little body warmth in; protecting him from the cold night air. And as he knew all too well, every little bit of body warmth helped.

The ground was tilting up ahead of them. It was a high dune, steep too. In daylight and with a proper compass, Beck might have considered going round the base of it. In the dark, with no clear sight of the stars yet, he knew there was a danger they would just start walking in circles as they stuck to the low ground. No, he thought grimly. Pressing on straight ahead was the only answer.

'This is going to be hard—' he started saying; then there was a grunt as Peter fell flat on his face.

'My feet were going *backwards*!' Peter said indignantly as Beck tracked back to help him up. 'The ground just slid . . .'

'Yeah, it does. Come on.' Beck fell in beside him, encouraging him up the dune. A dune was just a pile of sand with nothing to hold it together. All those millions of grains *wanted* to follow gravity, and needed only a little encouragement to do so. Encouragement like the feet of someone trying to walk up them. Every time he put his foot down, he felt it sink in. Loose sand cascaded down over his shoes with every step. And yes, as Peter had said, it felt like he was walking backwards. Two steps back for every one step forward.

'Blimey . . .' Peter gasped next to him. Beck heard the effort in his voice. With every step you had to lift your leg much further than usual, and it only got you a few centimetres further ahead. On normal ground the same energy would move you up a metre or so.

'Yup,' Beck agreed tightly. No more conversation was needed.

If the dune had just been a small hill they would have been up it in a couple of minutes. As it was, Beck guessed it took the better part of fifteen minutes, and he could hear Peter's heavy breathing as they reached the top.

'Break,' Peter gasped. 'Please.'

'Sure,' Beck agreed reluctantly. He didn't want them to hang around. The chill of the desert was really setting in, and if Peter got this tired after just one small dune, with the rest of the Sahara to cross . . . He didn't want to think about it. But he could see his friend's chest heaving with effort.

As if on cue, Peter's alarm beeped. They smiled and each had a swig of water. Even if they couldn't keep it in their mouths for very long, it still made sure they rationed the water carefully and made use of every drop.

Sitting on top of the dune, the boys could see a clear pattern emerging below them. Like waves on the sea, the dunes all tended to form in the same direction. One sharp steep side and one longer undulating side, sculpted by the wind.

'Hey, Beck, look!' Peter exclaimed. 'If we keep walking in the same direction across these dunes, we'll know we're heading in a straight line. You can see all the dunes are sculpted in the same direction.'

'Good work, Peter,' Beck said. 'Until the stars come up we can use these to navigate by – it'll stop us going round in circles.'

After another hour of walking Beck glanced up.

The moon had risen, half full, and some of the stars were out.

'Look, Peter, we can see the stars now,' he said.

'So which way?' Peter asked. His voice was a little less strained than it had been going up the dune, but he still sounded weak.

'Look for the Big Dipper,' Beck said. He craned his head up and scanned the heavens.

'You mean the Plough? The big saucepan?'

Beck grinned. 'The whatever.'

'It's over there.'

The constellation hung in the sky to their left. Beck had never been quite sure why it was called the Big Dipper. Or even the Great Bear. But you could see why it was known as the Plough. The big saucepan was even more appropriate. It had a long handle with a sharp angle halfway along it, and a pan with three straight sides.

'Look at the right-hand side of the pan,' Beck said. 'There's two stars in a dead straight line.'

'Two stars will always be in a dead straight line,' Peter pointed out logically. 'But OK.'

'Fair point!' Beck said. 'Follow the line up . . . four

times the distance . . . and there's a star up there.'

'Uh-huh.' Peter obediently followed the line. 'Got it.'

'And that is Polaris. The North Star. It's always in the north. It's not the brightest, but it doesn't move like the rest of them. So if you can see it – or, hey, if you can just see the saucepan – then you know where north is.'

'Cool.' In the dark, Peter's teeth flashed white as he grinned – a contrast to the strain Beck could still hear in his voice.

'You lead for a bit, buddy,' Beck suggested.

Heading down dunes was also hard work. In daylight it would have been no problem. You leaned forward and just let gravity do the job for you. You took long, plunging steps to keep upright but that was all. It was tiring, but it was quick.

But in the dark, all it needed was one rock they failed to spot, one misplaced footstep. Then one of them would have a broken bone and be as good as dead. They had a torch, but just one flash would ruin their night vision.

So, instead, they slithered and stumbled on

down the sides of the dunes in much the same way as they went up. Both boys felt the strain in their legs and the effort of staying upright. Soon their shoes were full of sand. Beck wasn't surprised. 'Get your shoes off, Pete, and empty them out,' he told his friend. 'If we walk like this for long then the grains will just cut our feet to pieces.'

They both spent a couple of minutes emptying out their shoes and dusting the sand off their skin.

'We're going to do this every half-hour,' Beck added. 'My dad always said that your feet are your most important assets. Keep them working and the rest of you will follow . . . Right. On we go . . .'

CHAPTER FIFTEEN

That set the pattern for the next few hours.

Sometimes the ground was level, or only sloped a little. Sometimes a dune reared up in their way and they had to tackle it like they had tackled the first one. And each time they did so, they were a little more tired than they had been before.

Light from the moon threw them into a half-world where everything was shades of grey. Darker patches loomed up every now and then – a rock, the occasional tuft of dune grass, the silhouette of a twisted tree. Mostly it was just sand.

Now that they could see the North Star, they were able to make a detour around the really serious obstacles. But the danger there was that they might veer too far off course and spend more time and energy than if they had just gone straight ahead. So wherever possible Beck kept them heading due north.

The cold soon started to attack them. At their next stop Beck opened up Peter's pack and they wrapped their upper bodies in an extra layer of parachute. It helped a little – silk is a good insulator, but not as good as a coat would have been.

'Why so cold?' Peter muttered at one point as they trudged through the endless gloom. There was a very faint tremor to his voice. Beck was fairly sure his teeth were chattering. He knew his own were.

'You're the physics expert. You tell me.' Beck thought he knew the answer but he wanted to keep Peter's mind active. It would take it off the cold that his body was feeling.

'Sand's a rubbish insulator,' Peter said after a moment's thought. 'It can't retain heat. It sucks it up during the day, which is why it gets so hot, and loses it the moment the sun goes down. The heat just runs away.'

Of course, Beck thought.

'And heat always passes from hot things to cold

things, and at the moment we're warmer than the sand. So, basically, we've got an entire desert sucking the heat out of us. Wow. No wonder it's cold.'

'That's why, when we stop to sleep, we'll have to put down a layer of something,' Beck added. 'Silk or palm leaves, if we can find them. Something that will insulate us. But that won't be for another couple of hours.'

'Oh, don't mind me, I'll just keep going . . .'

Peter lapsed into silence after that. Beck glanced sidelong at him in the dark.

He remembered Peter struggling to touch the bottom of the swimming pool. He had just kept working at it until he succeeded. So yes, Beck knew Peter was right. He *would* just keep going. But the bottom of the pool had been only three metres away. Their destination was many, many miles distant. The same stubbornness that made Peter learn to dive would make him walk himself into the ground. Beck had to make sure that didn't happen.

Finally a cluster of solid dark shapes loomed up out of the darkness. Their irregular outlines suggested

115

they were rocks. They surrounded a small depression, something like a small crater. Over to one side the trunk and leaves of a palm tree blocked out the stars.

'Time?' Beck asked. A pause.

'Four o'clock and I am beat.' They had been walking for over nine hours.

Beck hesitated, but only for a moment. Although he would have liked to press on a bit longer, Peter just wasn't used to hiking miles at a time and he could hear his friend's breath shuddering with cold. His own wasn't much better.

No, he reckoned. A rest would do them both good. Time to recharge. This was a good spot.

'We'll take a break here,' he announced. 'Then we'll—'

Peter kept walking. 'No,' he mumbled. 'Got to press on . . . Got to keep going . . . Can't just stop, Beck . . . Can't afford to—'

'Hey. Hey!' Beck grabbed his arm. Peter stopped without any resistance. 'You're allowed to take a break, you know. We both need it. Otherwise we'll just collapse, if the hypothermia doesn't get us first.'

'Wassat?'

'C'mon, Mr Biologist. You tell me.'

Beck led him over to the rocks. Peter's feet shuffled through the sand.

'Oh, that,' he muttered. 'It's when your body cools down faster than you can make warmth to replace it. You lose coordination. You go numb. And you die.'

'Got it in one.' Beck smiled grimly at the irony. The last time he had been worried about hypothermia, he had been frantically digging to avoid a snowstorm in the mountains of Alaska. Now he was in one of the hottest places in the world and hypothermia was still just round the corner.

'Wow. That could really spoil the holiday.' Peter's teeth were definitely chattering now.

Beck sat down next to the nearest rock; his friend dropped straight down next to him, hugging his knees to himself and shivering. 'I'll never complain when my mum turns the central heating up. Dad says the heating bills are too high – well, tough!'

Beck smiled, though he was shivering himself. 'Funny you should mention central heating. I thought I'd turn on some natural central heating.'

'Oh, ha ha.' Peter leaned back against the rock – and went rigid with surprise. 'Wow!'

'Told you!'

Beck lay back too. The rock was warm to the touch and he could feel the heat seeping into his body. It was bliss. He was cold enough that the slightest change in temperature made all the difference.

'The sun warms them up during the day,' he explained, 'and they slowly let their warmth out at night. During the day they'll just cook you like an oven. You shelter with vegetation during the day. But at night, rocks are perfect.'

'It works for me,' Peter assured him. He was hugging his knees to his chest and pressing his back against the stone. 'Environmentally friendly too.'

'Yeah, well. I'm going to have to increase our carbon footprint, I think.' Beck reached into his rucksack and pulled out the torch. 'Wait there.'

'What, when there's so much to see and enjoy?' Peter added ironically.

Beck chuckled and switched on the torch. He

flashed the light over the palm tree and nodded, pleased. It was surrounded by a layer of dead leaves and twigs. All bone dry, he thought with satisfaction. Not difficult to get a fire going here.

He crouched down to start gathering some up into a pile. His fingers brushed against a leaf; it moved.

Beck snatched his hand away. The leaf continued to move.

He slowly reached for a stick and used it to flick the leaf away.

Sitting in the middle of the torch's pool of light, like the star of a stage show, a yellow fat-tailed scorpion raised its pincers and tail in threat. Beck looked down at one of the most poisonous creatures in the world.

CHAPTER SIXTEEN

'Well, hello, Mr Andro-whatnot,' Beck murmured. The creature's full scientific name had appeared in the magazine back at the hotel but he couldn't remember it. But he could remember everything else he'd read about the creature.

The scorpion didn't advance but raised its tail. Maybe it didn't know what Beck was but it did know he was a lot bigger. It wasn't going to attack if it could get the same result – making Beck go away – just by being threatening.

Beck stepped a few paces back, keeping the torch on the little creature. It turned a quarter-circle on the spot and started to crawl away. Beck kept the light on it and picked up a stick.

'Pete,' he said conversationally, 'could you bring the knife from the bag?'

He heard Peter get to his feet and rummage in the rucksack. A moment later the knife was pressed into his hand.

'Geez.' Peter stood next to him and stared down at the scorpion. 'Is that dangerous?'

'No,' Beck said. He passed his friend the torch. 'Just lethal. Keep the light on it.'

He had to move around so that his shadow didn't fall onto the scorpion. It sensed he was in front of it and stopped. Again it raised its tail in warning.

Toxic as a cobra . . . the magazine had said. *Paralysis, convulsions, cardiac arrest or respiratory failure* . . .

Beck lunged forward with the stick and pressed the scorpion's body into the ground. Its pincers clawed helplessly at the air and its tail jabbed venom into the dry wood. Beck leaned down and, with his other hand, sliced off its tail with the knife. Then he cut off the head and pincers, and proudly held the body up for Peter to see.

Peter kept the torch on it and stared at it in round-eyed horror. It still twitched and its legs waved feebly for a moment.

'And what do we do with it?'

'Only eat it.'

'You're kidding . . .' Peter's voice was faint. 'I thought we were only stuck in the middle of a desert with no water and food. I didn't realize this was *I'm a Celebrity, Get Me Out of Here*.'

'Nah, this time you eat the scorpion and don't win a prize!' Beck carefully put the scorpion down on a rock. 'But they're full of protein and nutrients.'

As carefully as a surgeon, Beck cut the creature in half. Some of its insides leaked out in a pile of goo. He used the knife to scrape it all back into the creature's shell and held one half out to Peter. Peter took it gingerly and looked at it with exactly zero enthusiasm. He had even stopped shivering.

'Comfort zone?' Beck reminded him.

'Comfort zone,' Peter muttered.

Beck winked, opened his mouth and popped his half of the scorpion in. He deliberately closed his mouth and crunched, keeping his eyes on Peter's.

He saw the resignation appear there, closely followed by determination.

'Right . . .' Peter muttered, and followed suit. His face twisted as he bit down on the scorpion's shell. He swallowed with an effort, gulping loudly as he got the chewed mass down. 'It has a certain . . . something. But no one is ever going to call me a scorpoholic.'

'Well, there's plenty more where that came from. Now let's make a fire.'

Peter's enthusiasm was transformed. 'Now you're talking. You've got your fire steel . . . ?' he asked eagerly.

'Um' – Beck clenched his teeth – 'not exactly . . .'

Beck's fire steel was one of his most treasured possessions. It consisted of a short metal rod and a flat piece that looked like a blunt razor blade. They were mostly made of magnesium and steel, and when they were struck together they gave off sparks. With the right tinder, the fire steel could light fires in the jungle or the Arctic. Beck had used it all over the world.

Except that, right now, the fire steel was back in

their hotel room. Beck even knew exactly where it was: on his bedside table, between the lamp and the alarm clock. He could picture it perfectly.

'I *thought* we were going swimming, so I left it there,' he said. 'Funny, I didn't expect to be stowing away on an aeroplane and hiding from diamond smugglers.'

'So what do we do?'

'*You* gather firewood. A good pile of sticks and some kindling – dry twigs, old palm leaves, that kind of thing.' One good thing, he thought: at least out here, everything would be really dry. 'Use the torch whenever you reach for something – and poke around to make sure there aren't any more scorpions nearby. And meanwhile *I'll* try and make some fire.'

And so the boys set about their tasks, though Peter was slowed down by watching Beck at work. There was just enough light, and Beck had done this so many times before that he could do a lot of it by feel.

Beck was making a fire drill – one of the most ancient ways of making fire.

For the base plate he looked around for a chunk of wood about thirty centimetres long and as wide as his hand. There wasn't anything that exactly matched his requirements so he used the axe to lop a bit off a larger piece. It was thin, just a couple of centimetres thick. Near one end of this he used the knife to cut a notch into the wood. Next to this he cut out a small depression.

After this he had to make a drill and a bow. The drill was easy. He chose the straightest branch he could find, about a centimetre in diameter, and trimmed it to just over half a metre long, shaping the two ends into blunt points.

The drill was going to rotate rapidly in the small depression he had cut in the base plate; the friction would generate enough heat to make an ember.

To make the drill rotate he needed a bow – a bendy branch about twice the length of the drill. He cut a small notch at each end so that he could tie a length of parachute cord from one end to the other. He leaned on the bow to bend it, then tied the cord to each end so that it was stretched taut. The whole thing looked a bit like a child's attempt at playing

Robin Hood. But this bow wouldn't be used to shoot at bad King John.

Finally he needed a hand socket. One end of the drill would sit in the base plate; the other had to be held by him and he didn't want to drill a hole in his palm. He found a small piece of wood that fitted comfortably into his palm, again with a depression cut into it to take the drill end.

'How are you doing?' he called to Peter. Peter had assembled a fine pile of shredded bark, dried-up stems and leaves and some larger pieces of wood.

Beck nodded approvingly. 'Cool, Peter. You know, we could really use some good dry dung,' he went on. 'That makes excellent fuel. Smelly, but excellent.'

'Yeah, well, don't look at me . . .'

CHAPTER SEVENTEEN

'OK, let's give this a try.'

Beck used the knife to pry a slab of bark off the tree and set it down on a flat rock. This would be the ember tray; the part that held the very first embers. On the tray he piled a small handful of tinder up into something like a bird's nest, using his fingers to create a small hole in the middle.

Next he positioned the base plate next to the ember tray. A chip of wood propped it up at one end so that the tray slid under the notch. Peter sat the torch on a nearby rock so that its beam shone onto the base plate and tray. Beck then twisted the drill once round the taut bowstring, making the bow even tighter as it held the drill in position. Peter held the plate steady as Beck carefully put one end of the drill into the depression. The other end of the drill fitted into the hand socket which he held in the palm of his left hand.

With his right hand, Beck pulled back gently on the bow. The tight bowstring gripped the drill and slowly turned it. He pushed forward, more firmly, and it spun round in the other direction. Beck began to move the bow back and forth, back and forth, in a smooth, constant motion, while he pressed down on the hand socket so that the tip of the drill was pressed firmly into the base plate.

'You can just do this with a stick and a base on their own . . .' he murmured, concentrating on the bow. 'You roll the stick between your hands. Not as good as this way, and you get blisters . . .'

After that, neither of them spoke for a few minutes while the drill bit spun round in its small hollow. Beck knew it would be hot to the touch, like having a cigarette pushed into your hand. The friction of its movement would be boring out a fine layer of scorched wood dust.

'Look – there!' Peter breathed. Very thin tendrils

of smoke were rising up from the end of the drill, barely visible in the torchlight.

'OK, a bit more . . .'

Another couple of minutes and the smoke had grown into a much thicker layer. The wood dust would be fine and scorching hot.

Beck stopped and laid down the bow. He tilted the base plate and tapped it gently so that the glowing embers trickled along the notch and onto the tray. He then carefully tipped these embers into the middle of the pile of tinder.

'Come on, boy,' Peter muttered, as if willpower alone could light fires. Beck fanned the embers gently with his hand. Even blowing at this very early stage could be too much. They glowed a bit more fiercely and the kindling started to darken. Now Beck started to blow, puckering up as if he wanted to kiss the small pile. More wisps of smoke curled up and at last Beck saw the unmistakable flicker of flame licking across the dry wood.

'Yes!' Peter exclaimed, a triumphant hiss beneath his breath.

Beck swiftly put the flaming bundle on the

ground and started to add to the pile. Small twigs; slivers of dry bark. The *crack* as something in the fire broke in the heat was one of the best sounds ever, gradually spreading with the flame, consuming the pile as the fire grew. The boys huddled around it eagerly. With the fire on one side and the rocks on the other, still radiating warmth, their little camp suddenly became much more pleasant.

Another few hours, of course, Beck thought, and their little camp would be hell on earth. The rocks that were warming them so nicely faced south. There would be no shelter there when the sun was high – just heat and more heat, beating down on the sand and reflected back.

But they would have moved on by then.

'OK.' Beck reached for his rucksack. 'I think we've earned one of these, don't you?'

He pulled out one of the tins of fish, and Peter's face lit up.

'Oh, yeah! If it gets the taste of scorpion out of my mouth . . .' His face fell. 'But they pack tuna in brine. Salt water. We can't drink that out here.'

'This is spring water. It says on the label. No salt.'

Beck worked the tin opener around the lid. 'I love tuna, and man, am I hungry!'

'Even better with mayo!'

'You know, generally you want to avoid eating if you have no water. Eating fills you up but it also uses up precious fluids. You shouldn't eat meat without at least a litre to go with it. But with these' – the lid dropped off and Beck held up the tin – 'we can eat and drink at the same time.'

And that was exactly what they did. They passed the tin back and forth between them, picking tuna chunks out with their fingers, then lifting up the tin for a sip of the precious water. It tasted fishy, yes, but not salty. Beck could almost feel it soak into the dried-up tissues of his body. It gave them refreshment they badly needed, reviving them for the next stage of their journey. They could press on for a few more miles, even after the sun came up, before they had to settle down to wait out the hottest part of the day.

'This is—' Peter suddenly gasped and choked and doubled up. A chunk of food shot out of his mouth onto the sand.

'Hey, Pete! You all right?' Beck thumped him on

the back and Peter breathed deeply a couple of times.

'That went right down the wrong way. And it was solid.'

He poked the lump of food with one finger, then picked it up. He brushed fragments of tuna off what looked like a small pebble.

'There are stones in the tuna!' he said indignantly. 'I almost choked.'

'Let's see . . .'

Beck took the pebble off him and held it out to the firelight. It felt smooth between his fingers, almost soapy, even though Peter had brushed all the food off it. And it seemed to gleam, just a little, in the flames.

'So that's how they do it,' he murmured. 'That's how the smuggling operation works. They put them in the cans.'

Beck was holding an uncut diamond.

CHAPTER EIGHTEEN

'That's a diamond? Let's see!'

Peter took it back and studied it while Beck picked up the tin and poked around inside with his finger. There was still some fishy water at the bottom, which he was careful not to spill. He dug out three more pebbles like the first one.

'I told you the diamonds would be hidden in the tins,' Peter said smugly. 'But I thought they twinkled.'

'Only after they're cut and polished.'

'I wonder what it's worth?'

'Exactly nothing,' Beck said bluntly. 'We can't eat it or drink it.'

Peter gave him a sidelong glance. 'I wasn't thinking what it's worth to us. What's it worth to Mrs Chalobah? What's it worth to Sierra Leone? You remember what she said to us about using the diamond trade to help the country develop?'

'Well, yeah, but she's back there and we're out here.'

'So we need to let her know where the diamonds are, don't we?' Peter put the diamond down and felt for his camera. It was still in its pouch, hanging from his belt. 'I'm going to film it.'

Beck just smiled and rolled his eyes.

'No, really.' Peter looked sternly at him and Beck saw his determination. 'Put it this way. Even if we . . . you know . . . even if' – he swallowed – 'even if we don't get out of this, they might find our bodies and they'll get the camera. We need to let them know how the diamonds are getting out, so Mrs Chalobah can stop it.'

'Yeah,' Beck agreed after a moment. 'I guess you're right.'

He let Peter do the filming and record a brief explanation of what they had discovered. Beck kept quiet. He didn't want to voice his own thoughts out loud. The fact was, if every tin had a layer of diamonds in it, then they had less food than he had thought . . .

While Peter was doing that, Beck gathered up some fresh wood and kindling for the next night. They might not find any further on along their way. He put it into his rucksack along with the bow and drill. By the time they had finished their tasks, the sky was greying out and there was the tiniest hint of red to the east. Dawn couldn't be far off. They had rested, warmed up and eaten. It was time to move on.

Peter seemed to read Beck's thoughts when he saw him studying the sky.

'How much further?' he asked, carefully stowing the diamonds away in the rucksack. Both boys hoped they could get them back to their rightful owners.

'Probably just a few more miles before it gets too hot. But every bit counts. We have to press on.'

'Yeah,' Peter said heavily, 'I know.'

'Some tricks you ought to know . . .'

'Go on, my fine desert nomad!'

Beck grinned and kicked sand over the fire. He picked a charred lump of wood out of the ashes near the edge. It hadn't burned for some time and had cooled down. He spread the charcoal onto his fingers, then handed the piece of wood to Peter before rubbing his fingers beneath his eyes.

'You know you see sportsmen – American football players – with dark smudges on their faces? It reduces sun glare that reflects on your retina. Next best thing after a pair of aviators.'

'Yeah, I always wanted to try the Goth look . . .' Peter started to rub the charcoal on his own face.

'Plus, we're going to cover up our faces even more than yesterday afternoon. Just a slit to see through.'

'Suits me.'

'And . . .' Beck was grinning widely – so much so that Peter stopped rubbing and looked suspiciously at him.

'And?'

'When did you last pee?'

Peter frowned. 'What are you, my mum? Don't worry, I'll go before we start.'

'Oh, yes,' Beck assured him, 'you will.'

Peter started smearing charcoal over his face again, still keeping one suspicious eye on his friend.

'In fact,' Beck continued, 'we'll both go. In our boxers . . . and wrap them round our heads.'

The rubbing stopped. Peter stared at him with an expression that could have frozen a leg of lamb. '*What?*'

'It's moisture – it evaporates – it keeps us cool . . .'

'Can I just say, without the slightest shadow of a doubt and with all my heart, *no freakin' way*!'

'Way.'

'We *pee* on our boxers and wrap them round our faces?'

'It'll have to be our boxers because they're cotton and they'll absorb the moisture. It'll just run off the silk parachute material.'

'You are *kidding* . . .' Peter's eyes begged him. 'Right?'

Beck said nothing and his friend looked resigned. 'Distance to comfort zone . . . growing!'

Beck passed him the can of tuna. It still had some water at the bottom. 'Drink up,' he suggested.

They packed up the camp, then took their trousers and boxers off. They exchanged looks silently before putting their trousers back on, then turned their backs on each other and got to work.

'When we get out of this, I am so not telling my mum about this bit,' Peter muttered.

'What, you're not going to film it?'

'Stop it.'

Nothing happened for a long time.

'Tinkle, tinkle, tinkle,' said Beck, when the long silence grew too embarrassing.

'*Stop it!*'

'Sorry.'

'OK,' said Peter after a further wait. 'I'm done . . .'

He turned round to see Beck already putting his boxers on his head. Both boys burst out laughing. 'Do I look as ridiculous as I feel?' Beck asked.

'Yep.'

They laughed again, and Peter followed Beck's lead.

'My comfort zone is now so far away,' he said as he put his pee-soaked boxers in place, 'that light from it will take about a million years to get here.'

'It'll stink,' said Beck cheerfully, 'but it'll work.'

'So,' Peter said, and Beck could hear the

140

determination in his tone, 'off we go . . . and I hope to God no one spots us like this!'

Beck was looking at his watch. 'Remind me which way is north . . .' He already knew but he thought his friend could do with a little practice.

'Hold on . . .' Peter went through the procedure with his watch again and pointed due south. 'That way.'

Beck tried not to sigh. 'A hundred and eighty degrees wrong.'

He knew what Peter had done. The halfway point between the hour hand and twelve o'clock only gave you the north–south line. Next you had to work out which was north and which was south. The sun rises roughly in the east, so north has to be that end of the line.

'Oh, right, hang on . . . Oh, yes. It's that way.' This time he pointed in the right direction.

'If you know the time, then the sun's always a good guide. Early morning – east. Noon – due south. Evening – west. North, East, South, West – Naughty Elephants Squirt Water. That's how I remember it,' Beck said, pointing.

'Or,' Peter suggested, 'Never Eat Scorpions' – he paused – 'Waw! Almost raw,' he added as Beck laughed out loud.

Their spirits were up: it was time to get moving again.

They put on their remaining clothes and rubbed more charcoal onto their hands, which were now the only exposed part of their bodies. It was the next best thing to sunscreen for protecting their skin from the sun's ultraviolet. Last of all they took their mouthfuls of water, which they would try to avoid swallowing for as long as possible.

Their eyes met again, and for a moment Beck was in danger of losing the water in his mouth. He wanted to laugh. In addition to the parachute silk they now had dark panda eyes and pee-soaked boxers tied around their heads.

Peter's eyes – all Beck could see of his friend – suddenly crinkled. Beck guessed Peter was thinking the same about him. It was good to have someone with you – someone for moral support, someone in the same situation as you. Someone to rely on and be relied on by.

They couldn't speak with mouths full of water and Beck put the bottle into his rucksack and slung it up onto his back. They set off again into the desert beneath an ever-lightening sky.

CHAPTER NINETEEN

Walking through the desert by day was very different to doing it by night. The heat and the light were only part of the problem.

On the plus side, you could see where you were going. No slightly darker patch of sand would suddenly turn out to be a rock you could crack your shin against. You could see where your feet were going so you didn't risk twisting an ankle.

But now the boys couldn't see the stars either. It would be so easy to get disorientated as they trudged through the sun-baked landscape. You could set your sights on a dune in the far distance, but the land rose and dipped as you walked.

Landmarks sank out of sight and changed as you moved. And you couldn't be one hundred per cent sure where the landmarks were. The air warmed up as the sun rose – slowly at first, then increasingly quickly – and its heat began to reflect back off the sand. As the air warmed, it began to shimmer. During the hottest part of the day it would be superheated up to three metres above the ground and the shimmering would distort the horizon.

They set a pattern of walking for one hour, then resting for five minutes. 'It's a good way to keep a focus on your walking,' Beck told Peter. 'It gives you something to aim for. Five minutes' rest every hour: long enough to have a break but not so long that you start to stiffen up.'

At their next five-minute break Beck explained to Peter about the heat haze, which made it hard to navigate.

'OK,' Peter said with a shrug when Beck had described it. 'So we use the direction of the dunes to navigate, like I said. Shallow sides facing north-east.'

'Yes, but the trouble is, we need to be up on top of a dune to see the other dunes properly. This is why deserts are so disorientating.'

'Yeah,' Peter said. 'I once saw this film with two guys walking through the desert; they ended up going round in circles because if you're right-handed, see, then you're going to take slightly longer strides with your right leg and you'll go round in circles.' He looked chuffed with himself.

'Well, it's logical,' Beck admitted. 'We'll bear it in mind and keep a close eye on the dunes!' he joked. 'But actually, if you look here...' Beck pointed down along the ground. They were on a patch of loose sand that lay in furrows. 'These little ripples are effectively small dunes. They behave in the same way as big dunes. They are shaped by the wind, in the same direction. As long as you're crossing them at a constant angle, you're going in the right direction.'

He glanced down, noticing the brush growth in the sand. 'Look – there are signs of water here.' With his toe he prodded a small, stunted bush growing out of the sand. It came halfway up to his knees. 'Even these don't grow on nothing. There's got to be water somewhere here. Not enough for us, but there's water. If you see any kind of large vegetation, we're in with a chance. Look out for palm trees. The locals say they have their "head in fire, feet in water". It's not guaranteed – the water might be too deep down – but it's worth a try. Or if you find an animal trail, follow it; and birds and insects might fly towards water. They all have a better idea than we do.'

'Will do,' Peter promised. His jaw was set and determined, but Beck looked into his eyes and saw fatigue. Well, it was hardly surprising. It was now already hotter than a hot, hot day back home.

He passed him the bottle. 'Another mouthful and we're off.'

* * *

The stench of hot pee around their faces was bothering them both less and less. They were simply becoming immune to the smell. But their thirst was growing.

Beck wondered how much of it was psychological and how much real need. They had been walking for hours now, with only short breaks. Their bodies were using up water. And when your body was wrapped in searing heat and the sun was beating down on sand all around you, you felt you *ought* to have a drink. For some reason Beck found himself thinking of shampoo commercials. Beautiful people throwing their heads from side to side in slow motion while drops of crystal-clear water flew around them. It was the water that mesmerized Beck. Water, beautiful water.

He kept a close watch on the level in the bottles. There was only one direction it was going and that was down. And so far, despite all the clues he had given Peter, they hadn't spotted a single sign of water.

There was one other way.

He tugged at Peter's arm, and nodded over at a tall dune a short distance away. It was higher than all the others.

'We're going up there,' he said, his voice muffled by his face wrappings. 'See if we can see signs of water from above.'

Peter's eyes, hidden in the folds of silk, were a little glazed. But he nodded and obediently turned towards the dune.

It took half an hour to climb. Just like the dune back at the start of their walk, the sand slithered and crumbled beneath their feet. By the time they reached the top their thirst was intense.

They looked out over an ocean of sand, the dunes its waves and rollers. The horizon crumbled into shimmering air so there was no way of seeing how far it reached. It could have been a few miles away. It could have gone on for ever.

Suddenly Peter plucked at Beck's arm and pointed. 'Over there!' His voice sounded dry and wheezy – there wasn't enough saliva in his mouth to lubricate it.

'I've seen it,' Beck said gently. 'It's just a mirage.'

Yes, he had seen the silvery flash on the horizon too. Superheated air reflected light straight back to you, like a mirror. Your eye saw a burst of silver and your brain interpreted it: water!

'No, not that. Lower down.'

Beck looked at a point halfway between them and the horizon. Yes. Somehow his short-sighted friend had seen it even though he no longer had his glasses. A slightly darker line wound and twisted its way between the golden mounds of the dunes.

Even then Beck hesitated a little. It was due east

of them. It would take them off course. Sometimes dark sand was just dark sand.

But then a moving speck caught his eye. It rose up from the general direction of the dark line and circled round, then moved away into the distance. It was some kind of bird – he couldn't tell what. Probably a desert hawk or some other predator. No bird was going to live in the desert for fun.

No bird was going to live somewhere without water either.

'You're a genius, Peter,' he said. 'Let's go.'

CHAPTER TWENTY

The dark line soon dropped out of sight again as they walked down the dune. Beck navigated by the simple process of heading due east, keeping the sun on their right at forty-five degrees. The ground beneath them changed, becoming harder and more rocky. And then they were standing on the lip of a dry groove in the ground that cut its way through the desert as far as the eye could see. A hundred metres further along, the dark knot of an acacia bush clung to the side.

'It's a wadi,' Beck said. 'A dry river. It will only fill with water once in a blue moon, and only ever during the rainy season but . . .'

Peter took a couple of attempts before he

managed to speak through his dry mouth. 'Let's get down there,' he mumbled.

They stopped beneath a rugged slab of rock that faced north. The air was immediately cooler when they stepped into its shadow. Because it faced north it could never feel the touch of the sun and didn't radiate heat like other rocks did. They could sit with their backs against it, in the shade, and immediately feel the difference. They could take off their turbans and silk wrappings and – finally – get rid of the pee-soaked boxer shorts wrapped around their heads.

Beck couldn't help smiling when he saw Peter. His face was grey with charcoal, his hair tangled and matted, and he smelled of pee. Beck knew he was in just the same position.

'See how much good a nice walk does you?' he muttered.

Peter's mouth twitched in an attempted smile, but he closed his eyes and leaned back against the rock, looking drained.

Beck leaned forward and looked down the wadi. He could just see the acacia he had noticed earlier.

'Wait here,' he said, pushing himself to his feet.

'Yeah, like I'm going anywhere,' Peter mumbled.

Close up, the acacia bush was a tight cluster of dark branches and small, dark green leaves interspersed with thorns. These were spaced quite widely along the branches, sharp and curving like vicious claws. Beck carefully snapped a pair of branches off the main bush, and knocked the thorns off sideways. Then he took the branches back to Peter.

'Acacia,' Peter said immediately, though again he had to work his mouth first to say anything at all. 'In this part of the world they grow close to the Atlas Mountains.'

'Yeah?' Beck said hopefully. Instinctively he peered north, but down in the wadi he couldn't see the horizon, and anyway he knew what the horizon looked like. Yellow, big and shimmery. But if they were near the Atlas Mountains, then they were nearing people.

Of course, in a desert that took up a quarter of Africa, 'near' was a relative term.

A shrill cry from above made him shelve thoughts

about how near Morocco might be. Wings curved, feathers spread for maximum braking, a desert hawk swooped and touched down on a ledge above them. Peter and Beck weren't the only ones to seek out the shade it provided.

Beck took a step back with his hands on his hips. He could just see the collection of twigs that formed the hawk's nest. He studied it thoughtfully. The ledge was about four metres up, close to the top of the wadi wall, but there was a rock overhang just above it. The nest was protected from any threat from that direction. The only way to get to it was to fly – or do what most desert animals probably couldn't. Which was climb.

'Do you like your eggs over easy or sunny side up?' Beck asked.

'Huh?' Peter twisted round and followed his gaze up. 'You're kidding!'

'Nope.' Beck picked up his discarded turban, dusted it down and started to wrap it around his head again. 'Help me tie this on.'

'You realize the hawk will try and defend its nest?' Peter pointed out.

'Exactly.' So, wrapped in parachute silk, Beck started to climb up the rock.

It wasn't easy, but the nest wasn't high either. The hand- and footholds were good. *Keep three points anchored*, Beck's father had always told him: you had two feet and two hands, and you always made sure three of those were holding onto something before you moved the fourth: two to keep you in place and one as backup, he remembered his father always joked. Beck had his head craned back and his eyes fixed on the nest, expecting an irate bird to fly down and defend itself at any moment. And so he was lucky that the movement at the edge of his vision made him focus on where he was about to put his hand.

The scorpion was standing on a ledge level with his head. Beck and the arthropod were looking each other in the eye. The scorpion twitched its tail vaguely at him, but didn't appear to feel threatened.

It wasn't a yellow fat-tailed scorpion. This one was much larger and darker. But big was good. In general, the smaller the scorpion, the more potent they tended to be. And this one was huge. Beck didn't know the species, but that didn't matter: his eyes lit up. Scorpions, he knew, do not live in nests. They lay eggs that hatch; the young then cling onto their mother for a few months, until they are big enough to look after themselves. This one had five teenage scorpions on her back.

'O-*kay* . . .' he murmured. He made sure his feet were securely planted on a rocky ridge, and fished out his knife.

'Sending you a present, Pete,' he called as he extended the blade. 'Stand back.'

The scorpion raised its tail as Beck slid the blade under its belly, but then a flick of his wrist sent it flying out into the air. It landed a safe distance away from Peter and immediately began to crawl towards the shade. Peter instinctively scrambled back when he saw what it was.

'What am I expected to do with it?' he called up angrily.

'Put the rucksack over it or something until I get down. Right . . .'

Beck turned his attention back to the rock face, just as the mother hawk dive-bombed him. The first he knew of it was when he felt a blow to the back of the head; then he was half blinded by a whirl of angry feathers and beating wings around him. The bird screeched into his ears and its claws and sharp beak tore at the wrappings around his head.

Beck kept his head down to protect his eyes, which were the part of him that was most vulnerable to attacking talons. Sometimes a claw got far enough to prick him, but that was all.

There were three eggs lying in the nest. They were smooth and white, mottled with dark streaks. Beck bared his teeth in a triumphant smile.

'You're young,' he muttered as he slipped them into his pocket and the hawk flapped angrily above him. 'You'll have more babies . . .'

The bird seemed to give up as he climbed back down again. It obviously thought it had done its job in scaring him off, and the fact that he had its eggs was put down to experience. It sat on its rock ledge and glared down at the two boys, but it came no closer.

'We need these more than you,' Beck muttered to himself.

'Feast day!' he announced when his feet touched

the ground again. He produced the three eggs and waved them triumphantly under Peter's eyes. His friend was slumped against the rock, keeping a close eye on the rucksack he had dropped over the scorpions.

'Yum. Raw scorpion washed down with raw egg.'

'Fried egg,' Beck corrected him. 'Some of those rocks in the sun will get so hot we can cook them.'

He was pleased to see an answering smile – though it quickly faded and Peter slumped back against the rock. Beck frowned. Was his friend trembling slightly? It could just be exhaustion and dehydration. It could – worst of all – be heatstroke. Could that have started to set in?

Beck knew that Peter was mentally tough – very tough. But mental toughness would only take you so far. Ultimately you needed a body that was in good working order too. They both needed food and water. They needed energy.

Beck carefully picked up the rucksack and shook it out in case any baby scorpions had crawled inside. The mother scorpion quickly scuttled off, but he trapped her with a stick, then despatched her and her young in the same way he had the yellow scorpion. 'Scorpions and eggs it is then.'

CHAPTER TWENTY-ONE

They feasted on the scorpions there and then, crunching on the shells and sucking out the gooey mess of innards.

Beck immediately kicked across a long flat rock that was in direct sunlight and pulled it to the edge of the shade. It was almost too hot to touch. Carefully he cracked the first egg onto the rock. It settled, then slowly started to turn white. It was cooking!

'See – nature's stove!' Beck said triumphantly. Within minutes it was cooked through and Beck scraped it off with his knife and gave it to Peter to eat. He persuaded his friend to eat the second egg as well, which he hoped would pick up his strength, then wolfed down the third egg himself.

Peter still looked tired. Beck had been going to

show him how to find more water in the wadi. Now he reckoned it would be better if his friend just stayed where he was.

'Can I borrow your shirt, Pete?' he asked.

Without even enquiring why, Peter wearily leaned forward and took it off. Beck wrapped himself up again and ventured out into the bright sun with the shirt in his hand.

About twenty metres further on, the wadi curved off to the left. Beck knew that water flowed slowest on the outside bend of a river or stream. It drained away less quickly, which meant it had more time to pool and soak in. Beck had already scanned the parched ground around them for places where water could have collected – a dip or any slightly lower ground had potential. But the bend looked the best bet.

The soil there was dry and dusty. Beck knelt down and began to dig with a piece of wood; sand trickled back into the hole almost as quickly as he dug it out. He dug harder. Water would be found within half a metre of the surface, he knew, or not at all. If you had to dig down further than that then it wasn't worth the energy. You just went and tried somewhere else.

Beck grinned as he uncovered cool, moist sand further down. 'Result . . .' he murmured.

He spread out the shirt next to the hole and started to transfer the damp sand onto it. The stick wasn't flat enough to shovel sand efficiently so he scooped up handfuls of it in his fists. There was no obvious water but the sand was the same dark brown as the sugar his mother had once used to make crumbles with. It smelled fresh. Pleased with himself, Beck folded the shirt over the pile and looked up.

'Pete! *Get back in the shade!*' he shouted urgently.

Peter was standing halfway up the side of the wadi, bareheaded and bare-chested, unprotected from the sun apart from his trousers. The sun beat down on his fair hair as he craned his neck to peer short-sightedly into the distance.

Beck ran over to him and pulled him back towards the shade of the rock. To his surprise, Peter resisted.

'No,' he mumbled. 'There's trees . . . I saw trees . . . water . . .'

'No,' Beck said firmly, 'you didn't.'

But with a surprisingly strong yank, Peter pulled himself free and hurried back to the side of the wadi. 'It's out there . . . I saw it . . .'

Beck stared hard in the direction Peter was indicating, just in case by some miracle he was right. You never knew where an oasis might be. But he was pretty certain Peter was hallucinating. Anything that his short-sighted friend could see without his glasses on, Beck should have been able to see long ago.

'I'm really sorry, Pete. It's just not there . . .'

Beck spoke gently but he was thinking furiously. Yes, he knew a lot of strategies for surviving in the desert. He also knew how a mirage could trick the eyes. But no one had ever told him what to do if a friend became actively delusional.

Peter stopped struggling. He kept his eyes fixed on the shimmering horizon, but his shoulders drooped. 'It's gone. I could swear I saw it – I . . .'

He looked so forlorn that Beck felt a wrench inside.

'Come on, buddy.' He guided Peter back to

the shade. 'I've got something for you to drink.'

Peter sat listlessly while Beck retrieved the shirt from where he had left it – a bundle of cloth wrapped around the pile of damp sand.

'Tilt your head back,' he instructed. Peter did as he was told. 'Open your mouth . . .'

Beck held the bundle over Peter's face and twisted it hard. He kept the pressure up, compressing the pile of sand into a hard lump. After a moment the cloth went dark and a steady trickle of water squeezed its way through the fabric, forced out of the sand by the pressure he was applying. The trickle fell onto Peter's dry lips and into his open mouth. He smacked his lips.

'Mm! Best water ever . . .' His voice was almost back to normal. Then he saw where the water came from. 'So, just to be clear, I'm drinking water filtered through a shirt I've sweated in?'

'You're welcome to use mine instead.'

'Thanks, I'll pass. I suppose parachute silk's not porous enough.'

'Exactly. Here, take it.' Beck passed him the bundle. 'I'm going to get some of my own.'

He left Peter sucking more water through the cloth while he went back to the hole with his own shirt for more of the moist sand.

'Let's just say,' Peter murmured between mouthfuls, 'when we get back home I'm never going to look at a tap in the same way again!'

For a while after that they refilled their shirts with fresh wet sand and sucked on the bundles in silence. It was never going to be as satisfying as a good swig from a bottle of sparkling, clear water. There was also the danger of sucking a patch of the shirt dry, which just filled their mouths with the taste of dry, dirty cotton and made them thirsty again. But it got water into their bodies and it meant they didn't have to touch the reserves in the water bottles.

With a good supply of damp sand, Beck reckoned they could keep themselves hydrated until they started moving again.

After that they slept a little. They had been walking all night so their bodies were tired. However, their bodies were also very thirsty, which got in the way of a good sleep. But there was nothing else to do. They lay in the shade while all around them the sun turned the desert into an inferno. Sleep was the best option.

Later on in the day, Beck agreed to open another can of tuna. The water was good and the protein gave them energy. This one also had diamonds at the bottom, which they packed away with the others. Beck reckoned they had to be the richest pair of teenagers in the world, for all the good it did them.

He glanced at Peter as he tucked into the mini feast. The hallucination had worried Beck more than he was admitting to himself. Peter seemed mostly back to normal now, but every time they set out into the desert it seemed to knock him back. When they rested, he recovered a little, but he didn't regain all the strength he had lost. The cumulative effect was that he got slowly worse and worse.

Eating made them tired; sleeping after that was easier. At least, it was for Peter. He curled up on his side, using his pack as a pillow, and before long he was snoring.

At school, the official cure for anyone snoring in the dormitory was to whack them with a pillow. This time, Beck let his friend be. He sat up, hugging his knees, and gazed absently out of their rock shelter. For the first time he was seriously letting himself think that maybe – just maybe – Peter wouldn't make it.

'We need help,' he murmured under his breath.

Talking to the desert, Beck? Now you're losing it too . . .

No, he told himself. *Not to the desert – to whoever's out there.*

Believing in a higher power was encouraged at school. And his experiences, first in Colombia and then a few months later in Alaska, had taught him that it takes a strong person to reach out for help every now and then. At key moments in his life, forces he couldn't explain had come to his rescue. A wolf had shown him and his friend Tikaani where to find a pass through the mountains. And angels had surely guided him through the South American jungles.

He had tried to explain it to a boy at school. His friend had just laughed and put it down to 'coincidence'. And Beck had to admit that, yes, it *could* be coincidence, even though he didn't think it was.

The fact was that when he believed, coincidences happened. When he didn't believe, they stopped. When Beck's parents had been killed, he had prayed for help, and his Uncle Al had comforted him and taken him in. And Beck could feel his parents beside him. They had always had a strong faith, and at a time like this Beck wasn't too proud to ask for help.

And so he prayed. He was accepting that he couldn't do this on his own. It was a sacrifice of his pride. He hoped that whoever heard his prayer would recognize it as such.

'Please,' he prayed simply again. 'Please. Don't let Peter die.'

CHAPTER TWENTY-TWO

They broke camp again as the sun was going down. First they shook out their shoes and clothes and rucksacks in case scorpions had crept in. The sky was clear and the stars shone like diamonds, reminding Beck exactly why they had got into this mess in the first place. The North Star guided them firmly onwards towards Morocco.

The desert heat disappeared as quickly as it had come and the familiar chill set in again. Walking kept their minds off it, a little. Tonight, Beck decided, they would make camp earlier. Find some sun-warmed rocks, get a fire going, warm themselves up again. Give Peter's body every chance to recover.

The dunes still crumbled beneath their feet, and after several hours Peter's pace was slowing. A lot.

The next dune took the best part of an hour to climb; if it had been an ordinary hill they could have strolled up it in ten minutes. They paused at the top, looked at each other in the starlight, then started down the other side.

Peter took three steps, then fell forward. He rolled halfway down the slope before he stopped. Beck flung himself after him with long, lurching strides – just what he had tried to avoid doing after dark – forgetting the risk of breaking a leg on some unseen obstacle. He thought only of reaching his friend, a slightly darker patch on the dark sand.

'Pete? Pete! You OK?'

Peter didn't lift his head until Beck was next to him. 'Oops,' he said weakly, then sank back down again.

'Don't move . . . hang on . . .'

Beck patted him down, arms and legs, feeling for any bumps; anything that might suggest a broken bone. But Peter stirred and pulled himself up into a sitting position – something he couldn't have done if anything was seriously wrong.

'My legs just went,' he whispered. 'Sorry.'

His whole body was trembling and his voice shook. Beck couldn't tell if it was from cold or exhaustion or, quite possibly, both. Yes, he had decided they wouldn't press on as far as they had the previous night, but he had wanted to get further than *this*. They had covered a fraction of the ground they'd managed yesterday, but it looked like this was as far as they were going.

He helped Peter to stand up.

'Let's find some rocks,' he said gently, 'and we'll get a fire going again.'

They had to walk a bit further to find a suitable place. There were no large rocks like those that had warmed them the previous night, though they did come to a place with plenty of smaller ones scattered around – lumps of stone that varied in size from a cricket ball to something bigger than a football. Beck wondered if they had been dropped here by some ancient river or flood – and it must have been thousands of years ago. Just in time, he thought with a wry smile, to save the lives of two boys all these years later.

He handed Peter the torch. 'Keep this on me.'

By torchlight, Beck started to rearrange some of the rocks into a low wall. The rocks were warm to the touch, sending back the heat they had stored up during the day. Some he could pick up, some he had to push or roll along the ground. He took it slowly, using as little energy as possible. It would be foolish to build a shelter to keep them warm if it worked up a thirst that he couldn't satisfy.

Each time he moved a rock, he got Peter to shine the torch underneath it. They weren't the only ones in the middle of the desert who sought out the warmth offered by the rocks. They got another scorpion that way.

'Midnight feast,' said Peter. 'Yum.'

His sense of humour was still working, Beck noted, but his body was trembling.

Beck built the wall into a U-shaped shelter just under a metre high so that they could huddle against it, soaking up the warmth as quickly as the rocks radiated it. Along with the wood he had collected the previous night, he had brought his fire-making tools. With warm rocks on one side and a fire on the other, the shelter soon grew comfortably cosy.

To celebrate they each had a mouthful of water from the second bottle – they had finished the first some time ago.

'It's getting low,' Peter said simply. He held the bottle up to the firelight and sloshed the water around. The orange flames refracted through the water.

'Yup,' Beck agreed. There wasn't much else that could be said. Then a thought struck him. Right. He needed something non-absorbent, something that water would run off . . .

Got it. He pulled the rucksack towards him, peered inside, then emptied the contents onto the sand next to him. With a little effort he turned the rucksack inside out. The interior was lined with a kind of plastic sheeting for reinforcement. With the tip of the knife blade he started to cut away the stitching that kept the plastic in place.

'Anything I can do?' Peter asked, watching curiously.

Beck paused. He didn't want his friend to exert himself more than he absolutely had to, but he could certainly do with the help.

177

So he passed him the bag and the knife. 'You could finish this off,' he suggested. 'Get the lining out of the rucksack, keeping it as intact as possible.'

Beck got to his feet and picked up one of the pieces of wood that they hadn't yet burned. A few paces away from the shelter, in the dim light of the fire, he started to dig.

'You're not digging a well, are you?'

'Unfortunately not. But it should get us some water.'

'As long as it doesn't involve peeing, it's fine by me.'

Beck paused and smiled.

Peter caught his look and his shoulders sagged. 'It does, doesn't it?' he asked.

'Strangely enough, yes.'

When Beck had finished digging, the pit was about half a metre deep. He then took the empty water bottle and placed it upright at the bottom of the pit. Smiling, he then peed all around the bottle, making the sand damp with urine. 'Now it's your turn,' he said to Peter, who got up and made his own contribution.

'Right, that's the first part done,' Beck announced. 'Now for the clever bit!'

He then pulled the plastic liner across the pit, pinned it out taut with rocks and sealed the edges with sand so that no moisture could escape. Finally he placed a small stone in the middle of the plastic to act as a weight, so the liner looked like an upside-down cone across the pit.

'It's a dew trap,' he said as he returned to the shelter. He sat down next to Peter and they huddled together for warmth. 'As the air warms up, the moisture will evaporate and then condense onto the plastic liner above because it'll be cooler. And then it trickles down the inside of the sheet to the centre, weighted down by the stone, and drips into the bottle – clean and as if plucked out of the air – literally!' He smiled. 'Bedouin use the same condensation principle. They turn rocks over immediately before sunrise so the cooler surface gets condensation on it. But we'll be moving by then, so we do it this way. Simple.'

'So by the time the moisture reaches the sheet, it's just normal water again?' Peter said, getting it absolutely clear in his head.

179

'Yup. All the water from the pee evaporates and ends up in the bottle – by magic!' They both laughed.

'You know,' Peter said thoughtfully, 'there are probably people who would pay for this kind of holiday!'

* * *

They passed a slightly less cold night than before. The shelter was more enclosed and the rocks and fire kept them warm. They slept back to back. Once again Peter was asleep almost at once, but Beck could still feel the occasional shiver running through him. He knew, with a sinking heart, that Peter would wake up a little worse than he had the previous morning, and be close to collapse almost immediately. That was how it had been so far and he was showing no sign of improving.

And they still had many miles to go.

CHAPTER TWENTY-THREE

The boys staggered their way to the top of the dune and stopped, not quite believing what they saw in the pre-dawn light.

'Is that a—?' Peter began, and stopped.

Beck turned to him and grinned beneath his face covering. 'Fancy a lift?'

'I think its driving days are over . . .'

They scrambled down the other side of the dune towards the truck.

It was now the beginning of their third day in the desert. They had started out well before dawn, as before. The dew trap had yielded a little moisture. It was only about an inch, but their tongues and parched lips savoured every drop.

'Every little bit helps,' Beck had reminded Peter,

who just nodded. No, they didn't feel any better – but they would have felt worse without it.

Then they had walked on through the desert, ever northwards, as the sky lightened and the dunes emerged from the gloom all around them. Beck realized that Peter was pushing himself, always staying at least one pace ahead. He was determined not to hold Beck back. Beck had no idea what reserves of strength Peter was drawing on, but he admired his willpower more and more.

Then they had climbed the dune and seen the truck.

It lay half buried in the sand. Beck kept an eye on Peter as they approached it but he stayed upright. He had only fallen that one time. Beck noted the set look in his eyes and his careful, measured tread. He felt his own legs aching as well – more than ever before. But maybe their luck was turning. Beck's father had always said that dawn comes after the darkest part of the night. And certainly their situation was as dark as Beck could ever imagine.

A faint idea began to glimmer at the back of his mind.

The truck was ancient. Beck guessed it dated from the 1960s or even earlier. There were no tyre marks in the sand, no hint of how it had got here. The desert had long removed all such traces.

He had heard about the old desert battlefields of the Second World War – El Alamein and Ghazala. British and German vehicles left in the sand, still looking as new as the day they had been abandoned. Nothing rusted in the dry desert air and there was no mould to eat away at the seat leather. There was just the sand, blasting away at the paintwork and reducing it to a dull metallic sheen.

'Wonder what happened to the driver,' Peter said.

'Hmm.' Beck didn't want to wonder what had happened to the driver. Maybe he was lying a few metres away from them, buried by the sand. Maybe he had tried to head off on foot and been swallowed by the desert. He pushed the thought to the back of his mind.

The front half of the truck was almost buried in the sand, as if the vehicle was sinking *Titanic*-like into the desert. Beck thought briefly of exploring the wreckage for anything useful but guessed there was no point. There might have been water in the engine once, but that would have dried up long ago. The engine would be choked with sand; the cabin was half full of it.

But the truck's back half had potential. It was an old flatbed and had been carrying long rectangular crates made of wooden slats. Whatever had been in them was gone too but the slats remained. Beck got out the axe and used it to cut a good supply of straight, bone-dry wood. It would burn nicely at their next camp. Then he lifted out one of the crates and hefted it thoughtfully. It was about a metre wide, one and a half metres long, and had probably trans- ported livestock. The bottom was made of solid planks of wood, dry and light. The sides were slats and there wasn't much to the structure, so it was very light.

'Do you think we could both fit into this?' he asked thoughtfully.

Peter just stared at him as if he was mad.

Beck made the decision. 'Time for a brief rest. Pass me your pack – I'm going to need more silk.'

'There's not much left,' Peter warned.

They rested in the shade of the truck and Beck saw that he was right. With their shelter and their various wrappings they had got through a lot of their supplies. He didn't want to use their shelter covering for what he had in mind in case it ripped.

But there was still just enough spare silk to wrap around the crate, and enough cord to tie it in place. He left the top of the crate open so that they could get into it. Last of all he fastened a couple of lengths of cord, each about two metres long, to the front. He took hold of them and walked away at a steady walking pace. The cord tightened and the silk-wrapped crate slid along the sand behind him. There was hardly any friction.

'Are you going to tell me or do I guess?' Peter asked. 'And has this got anything to do with peeing?'

Beck passed him one of the towing cords. 'Only if you're easily excitable,' he said.

*　　*　　*

They kept walking with their new acquisition trailing behind them. It was light but it still dragged a little. Beck resolved they would try it once. If it didn't work then they would abandon it. There was no point expending energy on something unnecessary.

The next dune rose up ahead of them and they slogged their way up it. Having to keep one hand on the towing cord made it harder than before. At last they reached the top and looked down a smooth slope of sand into the next dip.

'OK,' Beck said. 'Experiment time. Get in.'

Peter didn't move. 'We're riding?' he asked sceptically.

'Yup. We're riding.'

Beck positioned the crate so that it was perched on the lip of the slope. Peter got in gingerly and sat at the front. He drew up his legs and gripped the sides with his hands. Beck stood at the back like the pusher of a bobsleigh, ready to give it the necessary impetus.

'. . . two . . . three . . .'

He pushed the crate forward and swung himself in just as it hit the slope. For a moment he thought it wouldn't work; it was just going to be too heavy. It slid slowly for a little way, but the silk moved smoothly over the sand and it soon picked up speed. Beck leaned back a little, moving the crate's centre of gravity so that the nose lifted and reduced the friction even further. Peter whooped as it picked up speed even more. Sand hissed beneath them and air brushed past their faces. They were cruising!

CHAPTER TWENTY-FOUR

The crate hit the bottom of the dune. It stopped so suddenly that Beck was thrown into Peter in front of him.

'*Oof!*'

They unpicked themselves gingerly and climbed out of the crate.

'You all right?'

'It's better than the log flume at Disneyland!' Peter looked a little unsteady on his feet but Beck was used to that. He didn't seem damaged by the sudden impact.

They looked back up the dune. The crate had cut a furrow of darker sand down the side. Beck guessed that at their usual pace it would have taken fifteen minutes to get down. It would have used up strength, wasted water, tired their legs and filled their shoes with sand. They had done it in under thirty seconds.

'*Can we go again, Mummy?*' Peter asked in a high-pitched child's voice.

'The very next time we find a dune,' Beck promised.

'*Cool . . .*'

They still had a good hour to go before the sun had risen high enough to stop them. Beck reckoned they could manage two or three more dunes in that time. They each took a mouthful of water to hold in their mouths and set off again.

*   *   *

Another dune, and another. They were all merging into one. Beck found he couldn't remember details of individual dunes because there weren't any. It was as if they had spent the whole of the last three days just climbing up one dune and walking or sliding down it again.

But at the top of the third dune – or was it the fourth? The fifth? – they could see a difference. The ground up ahead was much smoother. Still sandy, but no more big hills. The ground rose and fell gently. There would be no more need for the crate down there.

But, even more important, they noticed the horizon. It still shimmered in the super-heated air; it was still impossible to get a firm fix on anything. But something solid rose out of the shimmering and stayed there. Solid ground and craggy, rocky cliffs.

Beck feasted his eyes greedily on the sight. 'It's the mountains! It's the start of the Atlas Mountains!'

Peter came to stand next to him. 'Or the Anti-Atlas.' His voice was harsher than ever. Still not enough water inside him. 'Foothills,' he explained at Beck's enquiring glance. 'But yes. Basically it's the Atlas Mountains.'

They positioned the crate for its final slide. Beck took one last, happy look at the high ground ahead before giving it a shove. They wouldn't get there today, and possibly not even tomorrow. And even when they reached the mountains, they would have to get through them. But it felt like the end was in sight. Almost. It was like taking a long car journey and finally seeing a road sign pointing to your destination, even if that was still hours away.

But just then, Peter collapsed without warning.

They had surfed down the last big dune. Together they had packed up the silk, leaving the wooden bones where they were, and set off again. The mountains were hidden once more in the heat haze and the day was growing warmer but Beck had planned to give it a little longer before calling a halt.

Then Peter doubled up as if someone had slugged him hard in the guts.

'Pete?' For a moment Beck thought his friend had just tripped on something. But then he groaned and tore away his face wrappings just in time to be sick on the sand. He heaved until he was empty, then crouched, trembling, on all fours. Beck caught him just before he collapsed completely, then watched helplessly as he convulsed and let out a yelp of pain.

'Cramp . . .' Peter whispered through clenched teeth. His face was as red as a beetroot and he clutched at his thigh. 'Hurts . . .' He dug his fingers into the cramping muscles of his leg.

Beck helped him to sit down, then quickly grabbed the discarded wrappings and covered his head again, taking the opportunity to feel his brow. It was burning hot . . . and also completely dry. There wasn't a drop of sweat there. Beck's heart plummeted. No sweat, burning temperature, nausea, cramps, red face . . . Beneath his robes, so that Beck couldn't see, Peter had quietly been walking himself into a severe case of heatstroke.

The body cools itself by sweating. When it's so dehydrated that it can't sweat any more, it can't cool itself either. Peter's face was red because blood vessels near the skin had dilated, exposing more blood in an attempt to cool the body down. That was for the time being. Eventually he would start turning pale as his blood pressure dropped. Organs would fail. Unconsciousness would follow, then death.

Peter shivered. 'I feel cold,' he muttered. 'It's ridiculous. I'm *freezing* . . .'

I know, Beck thought gloomily: that was another

symptom on top of all the others. Shivering while you burned up, just like a fever. If he felt Peter's pulse, it would be racing – up to maybe 160 a minute. He didn't need to.

Beck looked at where Peter had been sick. All he could think was what a waste of good liquid that had been.

'Sorry.' Peter pushed him away gently, and tried to climb to his feet. 'Mustn't hold you up. Keep going . . .'

He swayed and would have toppled again if Beck hadn't grabbed hold of him.

'Journey's over for today, Pete.' Beck forced himself to sound bright and cheerful. It was so much better than *If we don't get help, you're going to die*.

'What? Here?' Peter stared around with blood-shot eyes.

Beck could see his point. Nothing but smooth sand all around. No rocks, no dips, nothing. 'I'll get the shelter up,' he promised. 'Get the sun off you. That'll cool you down . . .' It wouldn't help rehydrate him, though, he thought.

'What about over there – the oasis . . .?' Peter

gazed into the shimmering distance and took a couple of steps forward.

Beck caught him again. 'There's no oasis, Pete,' he muttered, though he looked around quickly just in case Peter had spotted something he had missed. There was nothing. Great, he thought, the hallucinations were back. He cursed himself for not doing something about this the first time his friend thought he saw an oasis. Maybe that was when the heatstroke started to set in. He should have done something *then*.

'Is too . . .' Peter staggered another couple of steps.

Beck followed him, desperately scanning the landscape for anything that could help. 'Look, Pete, we'll find the north side of a dune . . .'

'But . . .' Peter pointed pathetically into the distance at nothing. 'There . . .'

Beck bitterly remembered his little prayer of the night before. *Please. Don't let Peter die*, he had said.

He looked around again. There *was* something dark in the heat haze. He squinted: it looked like a palm tree. Tall and thin, topped by a cluster of spiky leaves. There was another one next to it emerging out of the haze. It was about two hundred metres away. How had he missed that?

'Son of a gun,' he breathed. 'That might actually be an oasis!'

CHAPTER TWENTY-FIVE

Peter turned a tired but triumphant smile onto him. 'See? Told you yesterday . . .'

'Oh, sure, you saw this yesterday!' Beck retorted, remembering Peter's supposed oasis the day before.

But even as they bickered, they were heading towards the oasis. Beck had to shorten his strides to match Peter's – even though his friend was trying to run.

Soon they came to a small depression, a shallow bowl in the sand. Somewhere deep beneath them was an underground river or aquifer – a reservoir of water trapped between layers of rock, pushed out here by some subterranean pressure to make this tiny patch of green in the middle of the vast desert.

There was a shallow puddle of murky water, no more than two or three metres across. What kept it from evaporating was the two date palms. They rose majestically, side by side, out of the sand on slender trunks, fifteen metres high or more. Each one was crowned with a clump of long, spiky leaves almost as wide as the tree was tall. Clusters of dates hung down between the leaves, wrinkled and luridly green.

The trees stood at the southern edge of the oasis and together cast their shade over the water. The fallen trunk of a third palm lay nearby.

A cluster of bushes bordered the northern side of the oasis like an untidy garden hedge. It filtered out the hairdryer heat of the north wind and turned it into a gentle breeze of cooler air.

To the boys, the oasis looked like paradise.

'OK,' Beck muttered to his friend, 'let's get you sorted out.'

The obvious thing to do was plunge him into the puddle and let him cool down, but Beck fought the temptation. The puddle was their only source of water and he wasn't going to pollute it. They had to drink it. They also owed it to any other living thing that came across this place, human or animal, to keep the water clean. But still, the first thing to do with a heatstroke victim was cool them down by every means possible.

He made sure Peter was fully in the shade. Not a single splash of direct sunlight fell on him.

'Right,' he said bluntly. 'Get your clothes off.' Out in the sun, clothes gave shelter. Here in the shade, clothes would just keep in warmth that had to be let out.

Peter was too dazed to argue. While he was undressing, Beck filled the bottles from the pool. They filled up with merry gurgles and bubbles that were heaven to his ears. Then he let Peter drink his fill, but slowly.

'Don't gulp it,' he said. 'Try to sip it down slowly. Let it soak into your mouth first. Make sure your body notices it's there. Really make the water *work*.'

Next Beck pulled out one of the bits of wood he'd taken from the truck and started to scrape a trench in the ground. It wasn't going to be big – maybe sixty centimetres wide and just long enough for Peter to lie down in.

'Burying me already?' Peter muttered, his face still flushed. He was still in the grip of his heatstroke fever. Despite everything, Beck had to grin at the sight of his skinny friend. Another flash of memory took him back to his adventure in Alaska. At different times, both he and Tikaani had had to strip down completely to get out of soaking wet clothes and avoid hypothermia.

'Lie down here,' he instructed, helping Peter down into the trench he had dug.

Peter's eyes were wide with surprise. 'It's really cool!'

'Yup. Go down just thirty centimetres or so and it can be sixty degrees cooler. Wait there.'

'Where else would I be going?' Peter asked logically.

Beck took the bottles over to the pool and plunged them under the surface. Then he went back to Peter and stood over him with a wicked grin.

Peter's face fell as he realized what was about to happen. 'Oh, no . . . !'

'You've got to cool down, mate.'

'OK, do it . . .'

Peter squeezed his eyes shut and Beck started to pour cool, life-giving water over him. He did it slowly and carefully, moving the two streams of water along Peter's body.

Peter breathed out in ecstasy as the water splashed over him. 'I will never complain about cold showers again,' he vowed. 'Cold showers are *good*.'

When the bottles were empty, Beck filled them up again and this time poured them over a pile of silk. Once the material was thoroughly drenched he handed it over to Peter. 'Stick 'em under your arms and your, um' – he gave a two-note whistle – 'privates. Those are your hottest places.'

He thought about soaking some more and draping them over his friend, but decided against it. Peter would cool down best with wet skin and a breeze, and he didn't want anything to block the airflow. So he refilled the bottles and again poured water over him.

Peter was soon looking a lot less red than before and his face was less drawn.

'How do you feel?' Beck asked him.

'Blinkin' awful,' came the answer, with feeling.

Beck grinned. This sounded hopeful.

He set up the shelter over Peter, ignoring his offers of help. 'If you want to help,' he said, 'get better. And that means you lie there until you do.'

Then Beck started to deal with his own thirst. Long cool sips of muddy, heavenly water. He soaked his turban and wrapped it around his head again. 'Heaven,' he muttered, and wondered if this oasis had ever saved any other humans.

CHAPTER TWENTY-SIX

Meanwhile Peter was lying in his cool trench, soaked by water, in the shade of a silk shelter, in the further shade of the trees. If *that* didn't cool him down, nothing would. So, Beck thought, next priority . . .

'Right.' He rubbed his hands together and looked around. 'Food!'

He looked up again at the nearest of the trees. The trunk wasn't quite vertical – maybe ten degrees off.

'Right,' he said again to the cluster of dates at the top. 'You're first.'

Normally, to climb a tree like this Beck would have just hauled himself up with his hands, wrapping his legs around the trunk. But a date palm like this wasn't just something you could shin up. The bark was made of segments – overlapping triangles. It was like the armoured scales of some desert monster and the scales were very sharp. Beck had heard of people shredding the skin of their legs, and other parts of their body too. So he had to work his feet into the gaps between the segments and climb up slowly and carefully.

It still didn't take long. From the top he looked down at the oasis, their little desert kingdom. He could just see Peter's feet sticking out from beneath the shelter. Then he did a full three-sixty, scanning the horizon in all directions. South, west and east – nothing but sand and heat haze. North – the mountains, a dirty brown ragged line reaching up to touch the sky. He thought they seemed a little higher than the last time he had looked at them. That meant they were nearer. Good.

Beck studied the clusters of dates carefully. There were three or four within easy reach. Their weight of a hundred or so dates made them hang down vertically. When they were ripe, dates were yellow; when unripe, green. And bitter. He picked the cluster that looked yellowish and sawed through the stem. It fell to the ground with a dull thud.

Next he cut away every palm leaf within easy reach. They fluttered gently to the ground.

'Huh?' said a voice beneath him. He looked down. Peter was peering out of the shelter.

'Lie back down!'

'Why are you cutting down leaves?'

'They're edible if we cook them. Lie back down.'

'You know, it gets really boring just lying here.'

Beck started to pick his way slowly back down the tree. 'Pete. Please. Just lie back down. I'll pour some more water on you.'

Peter lay back down in his trench, grumbling under his breath. Beck had to look away so he wouldn't see his broad smile. If Peter had the energy to grumble, that meant he wasn't dying.

The sharp bits of the palm-tree bark pointed upwards, which meant they dug into Beck as he climbed down. When he was low enough, he simply let himself slide round the trunk so that he was hanging straight down. Then he let go and dropped.

'We need some kind of container,' he said when

he was back on the ground. 'Not one of the bottles. Something fireproof.'

'There's the medical kit,' Peter said, after a moment's thought.

'Hey, of course.'

Beck had forgotten about that. He had taken it from the plane because it would have been stupid not to, but so far it hadn't been of much use for anything. But it was a small box, and it was made of metal. He dug it out and nodded with satisfaction. Yes, this would do. In fact, it would serve a couple of purposes.

Beck transferred the contents to a pocket on his rucksack, then got the axe and went over to the third palm –the one lying on its side next to its brothers. Sand had blown up against one side of it. First Beck used the knife to pry the bark away. He grinned at the sight of the insects and grubs that wriggled indignantly away the moment the sunlight fell on them.

'Oh no you don't,' he murmured, and swept them into the first-aid box. He held up the box and studied them carefully. The rule was not to eat any that were furry or had black bits showing through their skin. There were no furry ones but there were a couple that could possibly be the other kind. Maybe not black but certainly discoloured. Beck played safe and plucked them out again.

Pete's going to *love* this, he thought to himself, smiling.

CHAPTER TWENTY-SEVEN

Now that he had cleared a small patch of bark, he raised the axe in both hands and brought it down hard onto the trunk – again and again, until he had cut out a wedge of wood. He kept hacking away at the tree until he had enough of what he wanted.

'Even the trunk meat is edible,' he said as he went back to Peter, with a box full of insects and a pile of wood chips. 'We'll cook this too . . .'

They still had wood from the crates on the truck to make a fire, and Beck gathered up kindling from the bushes in the form of small dry twigs and leaves. Once again he started to use his fire-making kit.

Just as Beck was sawing with the bow to get the

first ember, he heard Peter gasp. Beck kept going but glanced up. His friend's eyes were fixed on something a short distance behind him.

'The sand just . . . *moved*.'

'Yeah?' Beck kept going – he didn't want to lose the effort he had put in so far – but he was immediately on the alert.

'And again. I thought I saw something.'

'Where, exactly?'

'About a metre away from you. Look – there!'

Beck glanced round to his right. He only had to turn his head a little way. Then he saw it. The sand heaved, for all the world as if it was water and a fish had just broken the surface.

In one swift movement Beck dropped the bow and the drill, and lunged. His fingers dug into the sand and for a moment he felt a smooth, lithe body between them. But he hadn't quite got a grip and it wriggled away. Beck swore and followed quickly after it. It really was like a fish swimming through the sand. It zigged and zagged its way across, with Beck crawling after it. Unlike a real fish, though, it couldn't dive deep. It had to stay near the surface where the sand was loose. Beck chased it halfway around the puddle, until finally he felt it between his fingers again. This time he held on firmly.

He carried it back to show Peter. It was a silver-grey lizard about twenty centimetres long. The pointed head had a wedge-shaped snout; the body was striped with bands of black and a dark yellow like caramel and streamlined with fish-like scales; the tail was short and blunt. Now that he had caught it, it stopped struggling, though Beck knew it would be off in a flash if he let go.

'Meet the main course,' he announced proudly. 'It's a sandfish. Not poisonous, not dangerous, and just what we need.'

He killed it quickly, holding it down with one hand and slicing its head off with the knife. He could just pull its guts straight out – a slimy, gunge-filled tube that he threw to one side, safely away from the water. He put the lizard's gutted body into the container with the insects.

'Not bad eyesight for you, Pete!' Beck joked, and went back to making the fire.

* * *

It was quite a feast.

With so much wood to hand, the fire was the biggest Beck had made since they arrived in the desert. They boiled the palm leaves and pieces of trunk with water in the first-aid box. Beck tried to think of a way of holding the box over the fire with something that wouldn't catch fire itself. Eventually he stuck three of the wooden slats from the truck into the sand, leaning against each other above the fire, and strung some of the wire he had cut from the parachute harness between the improvised tripod. The first-aid box dangled from this by its handle over the flame. He used the rest of the wire to skewer the sandfish so that it could roast properly in the fire's heat.

While the main course was cooking, the boys popped the grubs and insects from the tree into their mouths. They went down so quickly that Beck wandered back to the fallen tree to get some more.

'Fat, protein, carbohydrates and fluid, all in one handy bite-sized package,' he commented. 'Someone really should market them . . .'

'Limited market – trust me, Beck!' Peter said through a mouthful of sand beetle.

Dessert was dates – bitter but full of fructose and energy. Beck rationed these, even though there so many. He didn't want them to get the runs and undo all the good hydrating they had achieved so far.

The meal was washed down with all the water they could drink. For a long time after that they just lay on the sand, staring into the flames, deep in their own thoughts. Peter shivered. It was a genuine, proper shiver, caused because he really was cold, not feverish. His skin was goose-pimpling.

'I'd better put my clothes back on . . .' he said as he wrapped himself up again. 'I don't suppose we can stay here long, can we?'

Beck looked around. 'No . . .' he agreed. 'Probably a few more days if we had to, but sooner or later we'd run out of food. And if the water dried up . . .'

'But, I mean,' Peter said hopefully, 'someone would find us eventually, wouldn't they?'

'If by "eventually" you mean while our skeletons can still be identified by our dental records . . . well, yes.'

Peter said nothing.

'Remember that truck?' Beck asked. 'How long do you think that had been there? I'm guessing decades. But we were the first people to touch it since it got wrecked. The desert is so *big*. You don't just stumble over people. You have to go out and look.'

'So we have to keep moving,' Peter said with dull resignation.

'If you break down in your car, then the best advice is to stay put and wait for rescue. There are lots of stories of people wandering off to find help, only to be found dead nearby a day or so later,' Beck told him. 'But if no one's looking for you and you have no car, then you have no choice. You've got to self-rescue – and that means get moving.'

'Makes sense,' Peter commented.

'We can keep moving, with food and water, and have a chance of getting somewhere. Or we can just stay here until the food and water runs out, in which case we're stuck here in the middle of nowhere . . .'

'. . . with no food or water.'

'We'll rest a bit longer. We'll stock up on cooked

palm leaves and trunk. We'll fill up the bottles too, of course—'

'Will I make it?' Peter asked bluntly. It was such a sudden change of subject that for a moment Beck didn't know what to make of it.

Lots of replies ran though his head. *Of course you will . . .* was one. *Don't be silly . . .* was another.

He knew he would insult Peter's intelligence if he wasn't honest.

The rest and the meal had done his friend a lot of good. The heatstroke had done him a lot of bad. The good didn't quite make up for it. Add that to Peter's previous condition . . .

'I think we'll both die if we don't get our back-sides out of the desert soon,' he said simply.

'OK.' Peter met his gaze with a firm look of his own. 'You've talked me into it. When do we go?'

CHAPTER TWENTY-EIGHT

They rested until after midnight. It was the best night they had had so far in the desert. A comfortably big fire, plenty of water, the drowsy feel of full stomachs. They felt as reluctant to get up as if someone was kicking them out of their nice warm beds on a cold winter's morning back home.

But that was exactly why Beck reckoned they should get moving now. They had reserves in them to give them the strength to fight back against the cold of the desert night. They should be able to cover a good distance before the day warmed up again. They had cooked palm leaves in their bags and full bottles of fresh water.

Again they shook out their things for scorpions and Beck took one last look at the oasis. It was pale and ghostly in the moonlight. A smile tugged at the corners of his mouth. He had said that little prayer, and the oasis had appeared . . .

Well, the oasis had always been here, of course, he thought. How else could it be? But the fact remained: it *was* here, they *had* found it, and he owed his and Peter's lives to the God who had provided it.

The land sloped gently upwards to the north. It took five minutes' walking to reach the highest point. Beck couldn't help glancing back before they started down the far slope, when the oasis would be hidden from view for ever. Already he couldn't make it out against all the other shades of grey beneath the stars. It was like it had emerged from the desert to serve its purpose, and had now quietly sunk out of sight again.

He shook his head. There was no sense in harking back to the past. All they could do was make the most of the present and plan for the future.

They walked on through the night. It was still bitterly cold but they had enough food in them now to fight it. Every so often, as Peter's watch reminded them, they stopped for their five-minute rest and another mouthful of water. They were still using the Tarahumara trick that Beck had taught Peter, holding the water in their mouths for as long as possible. It kept them from getting unbearably thirsty, but thirsty they still were.

Despite that, Beck was feeling quite optimistic. He had seen the ground grow firmer beneath his feet, more like rock than sand now. They could make good progress without having to clamber up loose, sliding dunes. Walking on flat ground, in comparison, was so straightforward. Put one foot in front of the other, get into a rhythm, switch the mind to neutral and *walk*. You could keep going for hours.

And was it his imagination, or was that dark patch of mountains, low on the horizon where you couldn't see the stars, getting nearer? By day, Beck knew far better than to trust the evidence of his eyes. The heat haze could make the mountains appear near, but they never got any nearer. By night everything became harder still. So Beck had learned just to keep walking and ignore the whims of his imagination. He was concerned with two things: reality and finding people.

Dawn was approaching and the light was spreading across the flat landscape. Another couple of hours, Beck thought, and they would have to find another shelter for the day. This really was flat, he thought, gazing around. In fact—

'Hey, Beck!' Peter crouched down and ran his fingers over the ground. 'Tyre tracks!' He gazed up at his friend, his eyes shining. 'We must be near somewhere!'

'Don't get your hopes too high,' Beck muttered. He strolled on a short way, eyes fixed on the ground. 'Yup. More here . . . more here . . .'

In fact the dry, flat ground was criss-crossed with them, as if a herd of cars had recently stampeded over the desert. The noise in his imagination – the roar of engines, the grinding of tyres on the dry ground – contrasted strangely with the eerie quiet of the desert, where all he could hear was his own feet crunching on the dirt.

'I reckon we're on the route of the Paris–Dakar car rally,' Beck told Peter. 'Some French guy got lost in the desert in the seventies and decided it would be a good place for a car race. It happens every January – it's one of the longest, toughest car rallies on earth. So if this was January, we'd have no problem being picked up.'

'Oh.' Peter looked crestfallen. 'Funny. You'd have thought the tyre marks would have blown away by now. Got covered by the sand.'

'Look carefully,' Beck told him grimly. 'There's actually no sand here. We're on a salt pan.'

He should have realized, he thought. He had felt the ground grow firmer. He had noticed how flat it was. He hadn't put two and two together.

Peter looked around with casual interest. The dry ground stretched as far as they could see in the growing light.

'It's where the sea once was, isn't it?' he asked.

'Yes. But the sea water has long since evaporated, leaving all the salt behind. Over thousands of years it has become this dry, barren, featureless wasteland.' Beck tapped the ground with his foot. 'Nothing but salt, with this solid crust on top. But it could be worse,' he added. 'It's not necessarily the kind of salt you put on your chips; it could be caustic soda.'

'Caustic soda? I think we use that to clean the floor back home.'

'Well, think what it does to dirt on the floor, and then imagine it doing that to your skin instead. *Don't* get it on you. Either way, there's nothing here we can drink, no plants growing and most likely no animals either. *They've* got more sense.'

'Ah.' Now it seemed to dawn on Peter. No food, no water . . . 'What do you suggest?'

Beck glanced quickly up at the sky to get his bearings, and turned northwards. 'We get off it as quickly as we can,' he said. 'We just keep walking.'

But two hours later they were still on the pan and Beck knew they had to call a halt. The heat reflected back from the glistening, salty ground twice as strongly as it did from the sand. Any further and they would just roast.

He ground his teeth in frustration. He had so wanted to keep going. Another ten minutes and they might be off it, back on normal ground. Or they might still have miles to go. In the shimmering heat it was impossible to tell. Beck just couldn't take the chance of them walking until they dropped. They had to stop and take shelter as best they could.

There was no chance of scraping away even a small trench in the hard ground. There were no rocks and certainly no vegetation to offer shade. They set up their makeshift shelter facing west, away from the sun and also away from the steady north-east wind.

'The sun'll move,' Peter pointed out.

'So we'll move the shelter. But that won't be until the afternoon. And after that we'll set off again. We'll walk all through the night if we have to. We're getting off this salt, one way or another.'

The ground was too hard to drive the poles of the shelter into it. Beck didn't want to use force in case one of them broke. They had to pile small pebbles around the base of each one to hold it in place. After that they settled down in the shade of the silk and prepared to wait out the day.

The shelter kept the direct sun off them, and the wind, but it couldn't keep out the light. As the day grew brighter, the salt pan seemed to glow as the sun reflected off crystals in the ground. It shone straight into the shelter's open front and it seemed to burn into their eyes much as the salt would have burned into their skin.

They still had the silk they had used for their dune surfer. They managed to prop up a couple of slats from the crate in front of the shelter, and tied one end of the silk to them; the other they fixed to the main poles. Now the shelter had an awning that stretched out and down in front of it. It cut out a lot of the glare and made a bit more shade.

'Hey, we've got a patio,' Peter remarked.

Beck smiled, though he felt the skin pull on his dry lips as he did so. The task had occupied them for ten minutes. Keeping the mind busy was almost as important as keeping the body cool and watered. Unfortunately there were a lot more ten minuteses between now and the evening, when they could move on.

'I think we've earned our next drink,' he said.

Back inside the shelter, Beck held up one of the bottles and swished it about. It was still over three quarters full. They had hardly touched it since leaving the oasis.

'This will give us enough mouthfuls to get through the day if we space them out,' he said. 'Then we'll still have a full bottle to take with us when we leave, to get us through the night and until we find another water source.'

'It's going to be a long day,' Peter said mournfully.

Now Beck's smile only touched one corner of his mouth. Peter was right.

'There was once this old king,' he said, 'who asked his wise men for words of wisdom that would work in any situation. In the good times and the bad. The wise men went away, and they thought very wisely, and they came back and said, "This too shall pass." And they were right.'

'So when things are going well . . .' Peter said, frowning in thought.

'. . . then make the most of it, 'cos this too shall pass. And when you're having a really rubbish time . . .'

'. . . don't worry, because this too shall pass.

Yeah.' Peter brightened a little. 'I suppose that was quite wise.'

'And today' – Beck lay back on the hard ground and stretched, trying to be as optimistic as he could – 'shall also pass. Eventually.'

CHAPTER TWENTY-NINE

The day was a long time in passing. After a while they realized it was best not to talk. That just dried up the mouth. They couldn't venture outside because the heat off the salt hit them like a physical punch and the sweat started as if someone had turned on a shower.

Peter passed some of the time by running through all the photos and videos on his camera. Beck felt almost surprised when he came to the photos of the men in the hotel lobby, and the plane, and the diamonds in the cans. It had been three days ago. It seemed such a long time, so far away in another world, that he had to remind himself how they had come to be where they were.

The one thing to be said about the shelter was

that it was cooler than outside – which wasn't saying much. The day passed into a blur. A little snoozing, a little just lying there and looking at the glowing silk a few centimetres above their heads. All that broke the day up was the regular beeping of Peter's watch, announcing that it was time for another mouthful of lukewarm water, or a nibble of palm leaf and dates.

But finally the day was drawing to a close. The sun was low in the western sky and the boys were packing up the shelter. They loaded up their rucksacks and put on their silk wrappings. They stood there for a moment, two isolated figures in the middle of a sea of dry salt.

'One more drink before we go!' Beck said. They had gauged the first bottle exactly. Peter had taken the very last mouthful of water from it right on cue. Now it was time to start on the second.

Peter grinned and raised the bottle to Beck in a silent toast before putting it up to his mouth, sipping carefully. He then reached out towards Beck to pass him the bottle.

Neither of them was quite sure what happened next. Whether Peter let go of it early or Beck let it slip through his fingers. But the bottle dropped – as if in slow motion.

'No!'

Beck was already lunging for it, but too late. The bottle landed on its side and its precious contents splashed out onto the ground. Beck only lost a few seconds before he scooped it up again, but it was long enough. Just a moment ago the bottle had been full of water. Now there was barely a quarter left.

Peter stooped down, swearing as he helped Beck up. 'I'm sorry. I . . . I'm so sorry . . .' He sounded on the verge of tears.

Beck stared at him, at the bottle, back at Peter again. His mind was still trying to make sense of how it had happened. For a split second, part of him felt like screaming out loud. But he resisted. It had been an accident. No one's fault.

'What's your watch set to again?'

The question and his matter-of-fact tone seemed to pull Peter back from his guilt trip.

'Uh . . . um . . . thirty minutes.'

'Make it forty from now on.'

Beck carefully took his one mouthful and screwed the top back on. He put the bottle away in his rucksack, squeezed Peter's shoulder reassuringly, and together they set off across the salt pan.

They didn't talk. There wasn't water enough for that and there was nothing to say anyway. The situation was too serious for chitchat now.

Their one blessing was that the going was smooth. They were still on the salt pan. There were no obstacles, though there was always a faint chance that one of them would be too heavy for the crust of the salt pan and would fall through into the poisonous gunk below. Beck reckoned that if all the cars taking part in the Paris-Dakar rally had come this way, then the crust could probably hold two boys.

It took two more hours to get off the pan. The sun was well down but Beck saw the shape of the landscape change around them in the dark. He felt the difference beneath his feet. It was some comfort. All through the day while they had rested he had been plagued by the thought that maybe they should have pressed on just a little further that morning. But no, stopping back then had been the right choice. They couldn't have gone on this far in the blazing heat of the day.

The ground started to rise and fall gently. It was hard and rocky, scattered with fist-sized stones; still quite easy to walk on, and certainly easier than slogging up and down sand dunes. The boys just had to be careful where they put their feet.

Shortly after they got off the pan they were down to their last mouthfuls of water.

'I can wait.' Peter's voice was hoarse. He held the bottle up to the moon so he could just see the precious few drops remaining. 'I'll give it a bit longer. We should keep this for an emergency.'

'Pete . . .' It came out as a dry whisper. Beck had to swallow to get some moisture and try again before any sound came out. 'Pete, it's been an emergency for a while now. Drink it now. Just keep it in your mouth for as long as possible. Try to let it absorb completely. We'll just go without for a few more hours, then we'll stop a couple of hours before dawn and set up another dew trap.' He made himself smile, though it hurt.

'I don't think I've got any pee left...' Peter murmured, before taking his last sip and passing the nearly empty bottle to Beck to finish.

CHAPTER THIRTY

A night without water seemed twice as long as a night with. It wasn't long before Beck could hear the sounds of Peter faltering. The occasional missed step, the harsher breathing. Beck found himself constantly drawing a little ahead, just by going at his normal pace. He had to hold himself back. Peter was slowing down.

But he was still walking.

Beck stooped down and picked up a couple of pebbles. He rubbed them to get the dirt off, then handed one to Peter.

'Keep this in your mouth. It'll make you salivate.'

Peter silently did as he was told. Beck popped his pebble into his own mouth. It felt like it made a difference, even though it didn't. It wasn't increasing the amount of water in their bodies but it made their mouths a little wetter. Beck thought wryly: it made dying of thirst slightly more pleasant . . .

He tried to pass the time by thinking ahead. Water. They needed water. There was the dew trap he could set, and they would try the Bedouin trick he had mentioned to Peter – turning over stones before sunrise to catch the condensation. Maybe they would find more damp sand they could squeeze water from.

There were options. There were always options. There had to be, because if they didn't find anything, in twenty-four hours he and Peter would be dead.

Peter stumbled into him and sagged. Beck put an arm round his shoulders to hold him up. They kept walking, though it was hard to say who was supporting who.

Keep us alive . . .

It was a return to his earlier prayer.

What's it going to be? he thought. *Another oasis?*

As far as Beck was concerned, though, his prayer was an on-going affair. He hadn't meant *Please save our lives this once*. He had meant

Please save us permanently. Please get us out of this desert.

His prayers blended into his thoughts, his thoughts into footsteps. *Keep walking. Keep moving. Never give up.*

But they were slowing. Minute by minute they were getting weaker and more delirious.

A camel-shaped rock loomed up in the dark ahead of them.

'A camel,' he mumbled. Yeah, that would do.

A dead camel's guts provided an astonishing amount of water. It pooled between the linings of its many stomachs. Or you could cut open the rumen, the first part of the camel's gut where its food waited to be digested. The contents of a rumen were disgusting and stinking, but you could get fluid out of it.

A live camel was even better, because it probably had a human owner somewhere nearby . . .

The camel-shaped rock moved. It took Beck's water-starved brain a moment to realize why.

Then his eyes adjusted and he saw it really *was* a camel. It had lifted up its head to check the two strange creatures shuffling towards it out of the desert. It was tied by a halter to a small tree. A smaller dark shape next to it was a mule, which seemed equally suspicious of their approach. It challenged them loudly.

Hee-haw!

And the dark shape behind them was – Beck's heart sang – a tent! It was a larger version of their parachute shelter, with straight, rectangular sides. And suddenly the boys were transfixed by a powerful torch beam.

A man spoke, but Beck couldn't make out the words.

'*Salaam alaikum*,' Beck gasped. The traditional Islamic greeting: 'Peace be upon you.' At least he could remember that much.

There was a silence.

Then Beck stammered, 'We – we need help . . .'

CHAPTER THIRTY-ONE

'Hey, Beck!' Peter called from above. Beck squinted up. His friend was outlined against the blue sky, perched at the front of the camel's saddle. He swayed a little from side to side as the camel walked, then grinned down at Beck. 'I can almost see England from up here!'

The camel walked with an awkward, rolling gait. Its expression was lofty and superior, as if it had been personally responsible for saving the two boys. And even though it looked like it was wrapped in moulting fur ripped off another beast, Beck thought it was the most beautiful creature on earth.

He smiled: he was glad his friend was so much recovered. But the smile was a little grim because he had another immediate concern. The mule was profoundly uncomfortable.

The desert nomad, their rescuer, their saviour, sat behind Peter. He said something – Beck couldn't make it out. Peter replied and the man laughed.

The man was called Anwar and he was a Berber. Beck had worked that much out. He had a dark moustache and shrewd eyes, thoughtful but friendly, set in a tanned, weathered face. Because of his headscarf that was about all they could see of his features.

Some time during the previous twenty-four hours they must have crossed the invisible border into Morocco. This part of North Africa had once been run jointly by Spain and France, and Anwar spoke French with a heavy Berber accent. This didn't help Beck at all, who had enough difficulty following French with a French accent. They could communicate a few words but that was all.

It was pure fluke that Anwar had been where he was. Fluke or fate. He had intended to be back at his village by now. He was a trader, carrying goods across the desert. His mule had picked up a limp –

a thorn in his foot, which Anwar had removed – and he was giving it a day to get better before he finished the journey.

Anwar's instincts as a desert dweller had taken over the moment the boys stumbled out of the desert. He had given them water out of a chipped enamel bowl decorated with geometric designs. Peter had tried to get the entire bowlful down in a couple of seconds. Anwar had stopped him gently and shown him how to sip it slowly. Give the water time to absorb, to soak in. It really would be counter-productive to drink it so fast that your body rejected it and you threw it back up again. That water had been the sweetest taste Beck had ever had in his mouth.

After the water, camel milk. Not so long ago this had been inside the camel, though Anwar served it from a bottle made of goatskin. It was thick and creamy and energy-giving. Then, with their stomachs satisfied, Anwar had let them nibble some solid food – some rough bread and bits of cooked meat.

'What, no scorpion?' Peter had mumbled sleepily. Not long after that, he and Beck were both rolled up in a pair of rugs and slumbering in a corner of the tent. The tent wasn't really large enough for the three of them and Anwar insisted on sleeping outside, by the fire. This embarrassed them no end, but Beck knew it was simply the Berber way. When it came to hospitality, guests took priority. It was their custom, and Beck and Peter acknowledged it gratefully with their hands held together in front of their faces, as if praying. Anwar smiled warmly and left them alone in the tent.

That night they slept like babies, warm, fed and safe.

Anwar's village was about five miles away, he told them. By dawn the camp had been packed up and stowed on the back and sides of the camel, along with all his trade goods. The camel saddle was like a square four-legged stool with curved legs, and it perched in front of the camel's hump. It really didn't look like it should stay there, but it did. That was where Anwar and Peter now rode, while Beck took the mule. It had a very sharp backbone which seemed to be very slowly sawing him in half. He almost felt he would rather be walking . . .

The village came into view a couple of hours later. It emerged out of the heat haze with the Atlas Mountains looming large above it. Walls built out of sand-coloured blocks of stone surrounded low, single-storey dwellings. At first glance it looked almost deserted – no one was moving around outside much in the heat of the day.

But there was life. Here a woman carrying a basket, there a couple of children playing in the shade of a wall. A short distance away a small group of men armed with sticks wandered casually around the outskirts of the village.

'What are they doing?' Peter called down.

'Snake hunting,' Beck guessed. 'They probably do it all the time.'

Unexpectedly, Anwar added a comment. It sounded like 'Ser-pon', followed by another torrent of words that Beck couldn't make out.

'That's "snake" in French,' Peter translated. His French was proving much better than Beck's. '*Serpent* means snake.'

'Well, this village is here because there's shade and food and water,' Beck told him, 'so of course the snakes come here too. There's one particular kind of snake, the horned viper, that's especially hard to spot. It hides in the sand with just its eyes showing, and it's sand-coloured. I heard once of a child who got bitten on the finger, and to save his life they had to cut the finger off right away before his blood could carry the venom into his heart.'

As they approached the village, they heard the men calling to each other excitedly. 'Looks like they might have one, Beck!' Peter shouted.

CHAPTER THIRTY-TWO

The men spread out to surround a bush, jabbing at the ground around it with their sticks. One of them darted forward suddenly and pressed his stick to the ground, while another drew a knife and slashed down with it. A moment later the second man held up a thin, wriggling form about half a metre long.

Another couple of villagers started to dig with their sticks.

'They'll bury the head,' Beck told Peter. 'It can still bite out of reflex.'

'And I suppose we get to eat the body,' Peter said, sounding none too enthusiastic.

'Probably not – which is a shame because roast snake is a lot nicer than roast scorpion! They would think of it like eating a dead enemy. They'll treat it with great respect.'

Soon other villagers started to appear, drawn towards the new arrivals. The snake hunters drifted over as well. Presumably they all knew Anwar and had been expecting him back. But his appearance out of the desert accompanied by two European boys was arousing great curiosity. By the time the camel and the mule reached the edge of the village there was quite a crowd to meet them.

The village looked like it had barely changed in the last thousand years. There were clues here and there, though. One of the houses had some sort of aerial on the roof; Beck couldn't see anything that looked like a telephone line, but you never knew. Hope was rising within him. It only took one person with a mobile phone or radio, and they could be back in touch with the world again. Someone could even get word to Uncle Al about where they were.

They were taken into a hut that was one of a pair of buildings in a small enclosure. There they were left with a change of clothes – boy-sized Berber robes – and pots of water, and the very strong hint that they should wash before anything else. Beck dreaded to think how they must smell. They grabbed the opportunity.

When they were done there was a polite tap at the door. Anwar poked his head in and beckoned to them. They followed him outside, feeling a little self-conscious in their new clothes. Waiting modestly outside was a woman about the same age as Mrs Chalobah.

'I understand you are British, yes?' she asked in English. She smiled when she saw their reaction of surprise and relief. 'I am Tahiyah. I have son who work near coast,' she explained. 'Many English tourists. I have work myself sometimes there. You tell how you come here?'

And so they told their story, sitting in the shade of a tree, sipping sweet tea and eating a kind of wafer soaked in butter and honey.

Their story was received with much gesturing and exclamations at all the key moments. When they mentioned the oasis, there was a lot of wise nodding and nudging each other, though Beck wasn't sure why. He was more interested to see that he had guessed right about the phones. Even before they finished talking, he saw at least two guys take phones from their robes and go off a short distance, where they relayed the story with many grand gestures and, Beck suspected, a lot of exaggeration.

One man came and tapped Tahiyah on the shoulder and whispered into her ear. She smiled a broad smile at the two boys.

'We are talk to police in Marrakech,' she said. 'They are come tomorrow to find you. They say they hear about two boys missing. They say they amaze you alive!'

'Yup,' Beck said. He didn't want to mention the doubt in his heart.

Peter glanced sidelong at him. 'What is it, Beck?'

Beck looked back at him in surprise. 'What's what?'

'There's something bothering you.'

Beck sighed. 'Well, all those guys jabbering away on their phones . . . Who else has heard we're here?'

'How do you mean?'

'I remember what Mrs Chalobah said about the

smugglers. She said, "Their web of evil spreads over the entire continent." We're still on the continent, Pete. I'm just worried that it won't just be the good guys who come to find us.'

'Do not worry!' Tahiyah exclaimed. Beck started: they had been talking quietly and he hadn't expected her to follow their conversation. 'You do not worry. We do not welcome thieves!'

Beck smiled. He appreciated her reassuring words. But these were good, kind people and he didn't want to bring any trouble down on them. The sooner they were safe with the Marrakech police, the better. But that wouldn't be until tomorrow. And a lot could happen in the desert in twenty-four hours.

*   *   *

The rest of the day passed in a blur. They tried to teach some English words to the crowd of children who followed them everywhere, but the kids just cracked up with laughter whenever they heard Peter and Beck's English accents. The wonderful atmosphere in the village – the feeling of warmth and respect wherever they went – did them more good than a week's holiday. It was exactly what they needed to help their recovery – along with the endless supply of sweet tea and local delicacies.

Later in the day they set out to explore the rest of the village. Peter was back in journalist mode. He wanted to capture the place from every angle.

The hut where they had changed seemed to be the village guest house, and it was their temporary home.

'I wonder what's in here?' Peter said as they passed one of the other small rooms in their enclosure.

'*No!*' Beck yelped, but Peter had pushed the door open and peered in before he could stop him. It was full of pots and pans and bits of junk. The place was obviously used for storage.

Peter looked round at his friend, puzzled. 'What?'

Beck crouched down and pointed at some wavy lines on the ground. They were etched into the top layer of sand next to the door. '*That* is a snake track.'

Peter looked in horror at the hut he had been about to enter, then backed quickly away.

'They'll have swept this whole area clean this morning,' Beck went on, 'but a snake has definitely been here at some point.' He examined the track more closely. 'Basically, don't go in after dark.'

'We only sleep next door!' Peter protested, pointing at their hut.

'So we'll shut our door. We'll be OK,' Beck insisted.

Finally the day was over and it was time to turn in. At the entrance to the enclosure they said goodnight to Tahiyah and Anwar and all their new friends, and went into their hut.

Peter was asleep almost immediately. For a while Beck lay on the floor on his bed of coarse rugs and watched the moonlight from the window move across the ceiling. Endless thoughts turned over in his mind.

After a while he got up and fumbled in his rucksack for the torch and a couple of other items. Then he cautiously let himself out of the hut again. He followed his own advice and kept the torch beam on the ground, looking out for snakes.

Five minutes later he was back in bed again, his mind put at rest. This time he rolled over and was soon asleep himself.

CHAPTER THIRTY-THREE

A metallic crash awoke him. It was loud and clanging, like a pile of saucepans falling to the ground. Beck knew exactly what it was.

He was awake in a moment. He leaped out of bed and crouched by the window, then slowly raised his head so he could peer over the sill.

Just before going to sleep, he had stretched a length of parachute cord at knee height across the entrance to the enclosure. At either end, out of sight of anyone entering from outside, he had tied a pot from the shed. Then he had piled a couple more on top. Anyone who walked into the enclosure would snag the line and dislodge the pots. And that was exactly what had happened.

The figure of a man crouched at the entrance.

Beck couldn't see him clearly but the outline of his clothes said he wasn't a Berber. The muffled swearing in Afrikaans helped identify him. Beck was almost certain it was the South African from the plane.

His instinct had been right. Word about them had spread.

Beck took a deep breath. If he shouted out loud enough, someone would hear. What was French for 'help'? Oh yes – *Au secours!* People would come. But just then the man brought his hand up to chest level and Beck saw moonlight glint on a gun barrel. Yes, someone would come, but the man would still have plenty of time to shoot Beck and Peter – and anyone else who came running. Beck would have to do this on his own.

He bit his lip and reached slowly for the axe. He had left it by his bed. His fingers closed around the handle and he sidled over to the door. The man would come in. Beck would have to hit him hard. It wasn't something he had ever done before and he only intended to use the flat of the blade. But it was the man or him.

Peter stirred and mumbled. In a flash Beck was

by his side, pressing his finger against his lips. Peter's eyes widened, but he stayed quiet. Beck went back to the window, as close as he dared, and peered out.

It took a moment to spot the man again. Beck's heart pounded.

The man had crept over to the other hut, the one used for storage. He had a fifty-fifty chance of choosing theirs, but luckily he'd chosen the other one and disappeared inside.

A pause.

Another pause. And then—

An ear-splitting scream. The man staggered backwards out of the hut, clutching at his leg, and toppled over. The gun flew out of his grasp and landed on the sand some way from where he'd fallen. He tried to stand, but fell again, screaming in agony.

A line of wriggling darkness flowed out of the shed after him. The snake was trapped between the hut and the man on the ground – and a cornered snake is lethal. It raised its head and Beck recognized the outline. This wasn't a horned viper, the snake he had described to Peter. There was no mistaking the hood that swelled out from its head. This was a cobra, one of the most recognizable and deadly snakes in the world.

Beck didn't think twice. He leaped out of the hut with the axe held high and brought it down on the snake. The reptile was sliced in two before it could bite the man again. He used the blade to flick the severed head into a dark corner of the enclosure. Then, chest heaving and still clutching the axe, he stood over the fallen man. For a moment they stared at each other, potential murderer and intended victim.

'Help me . . .' the man gasped.

For a moment Beck just wanted to shout, *No!* But he knew he couldn't do that. He was better than this villain.

Peter was now standing in the doorway to the hut. 'What is it? What happened?'

Beck came to a decision. 'Bring the torch, and the rucksack.' And then to the man: 'Where did it get you?'

'Back of the leg . . .' the man gasped through gritted teeth, rolling on the ground in agony.

'Turn over and stay still.'

A moment later Peter had come back with the rucksack. He kept the torch beam on the fallen man while Beck rolled up the leg of his trousers. The bite marks were plain to see in his calf: two dark holes, welling with blood and already swelling up.

Beck hardly noticed as villagers gathered round. They would all have been woken by the racket the South African had made. Beck ignored them as he delved into the pocket of the rucksack for the contents of the medical kit. There was no time to lose.

'Don't move,' Beck muttered. 'It'll just spread the poison.'

The South African was ashen with shock and pain; he clenched his teeth.

'So' – Peter seemed fascinated and horrified at the same time – 'are you going to cut the bite? Suck out the poison? Put on a tourniquet?'

'You've seen too many movies.' Beck fished out a gauze pad and a length of bandage.

Beck pressed the pad firmly over the bite and started to wrap the bandage round and round the leg. 'A tourniquet just blocks the blood flow. You could end up losing a limb. This just needs firm pressure to slow the release of the venom until we get him to a hospital. He was lucky, sort of. A cobra's poison is neurotoxic, not haemotoxic like the viper's. It attacks the nerves, not the blood, and he got bitten in the fleshy part of his leg. If he stays still, he could live.'

'*Could live*? What do you mean, *Could live*?' the man gasped.

'Depends on how you react and whether or not the snake gave you a dry bite or not,' Beck replied. He looked at the wound marks again carefully. 'Looks like only two puncture marks. That means it might not have injected you with venom – you got a dry bite. If there's a third puncture, that's the injected venom. You might have got lucky.'

The South African grimaced in pain again. 'You bloody kids. If I die then you die too.' He made a lunge to try and reach his gun in the dark, but Peter grabbed it first.

Beck looked at the man angrily. 'I know who you are. You smuggle diamonds and ruin lives in the process. When do people stop mattering more than lumps of stone that you dig out of the ground?' Beck demanded. 'Is it getting rich? Is that all you care about? 'Cos let me tell you, if I was rich there's no way I'd end up lying face down in the dirt letting a boy half my age save my life.' Beck stared him right in the eye. 'How many people have lost their lives because of you? And I don't mean one or two. I mean, how many thousands have died because of what you've stolen?'

'Oh, spare me the sermon,' the man snarled.

'Well, you'll have plenty of time to think about it in jail, won't you?' Beck muttered.

'Jail?' Now the man sneered through his pain. 'I'm not going to jail.'

This time Beck stopped winding the bandage round and stared at him in disbelief. 'Why? You came here tonight to kill us. We have witnesses.'

'I don't think so. I'm a tourist who got lost. My car is nearby. I was looking for help.'

'You have a gun!' Peter put in.

'So what? It's not the safest country.'

'We saw you in Sierra Leone! In a plane full of smuggled diamonds!'

'Too true, kid. You knew about the diamond-smuggling – that's why I hoped the desert would have killed you – and spared me the job of coming here to finish this.'

Beck and Peter both opened their mouths to speak at the same time.

'So whose word will the police take?' the man asked them. 'An innocent tourist's, or the ramblings of two kids?'

'But you just confessed!'

'Only to you two.' The man lifted his head slightly to address the witnesses. 'Hello, anybody? Does anyone here speak English? Anyone at all?' He was smiling.

Beck stared at the crowd, trying in vain to pick out Tahiyah. But she wasn't there. It was just the men of the village, and none of them spoke a word of English.

Beck's heart pounded and he almost felt sick.

This man had come to kill them. He had saved this man's life because it was the right thing to do. This man had just confessed to everything. And there was nothing they could do about it. Was he going to get away with it?

But another voice was speaking and it took Beck a moment to work out who it was. It was the man again.

'*Too true, kid. You know about the diamond-smuggling – that's why I hoped the desert would have killed you – and spared me the job of coming here to finish this.*'

The voice was tinny but it could be understood perfectly. It was coming out of the microphone of Peter's camera. Peter switched it off and beamed triumphantly at Beck, while still pointing the gun at the smuggler. Beck slowly grinned back, not quite daring to believe it.

And the man let his head drop back down to the ground and let out a howl of pain, anger and frustration.

CHAPTER THIRTY-FOUR

Early the next morning two Toyota Land Cruisers drove out of the desert. They both had police markings.

A couple of policemen and a medic got out of the first one. They had words with the village chief and then disappeared into the hut where the South African was being held. The villagers had taken turns watching over him to make sure he didn't escape. Not that this was likely in his weakened state.

From the other car stepped a more senior-looking policeman, along with his assistant – and Uncle Al. Al didn't say a word as he walked up to the grinning boys. He just pulled Beck hard into an embrace that squeezed the air out of him.

'I can't leave you alone for a second, can I, Beck?' he said gruffly.

'Told you he'd say that . . .' Peter remarked.

Later, they had to tell their story again. Not only for Al's benefit, but also as an official statement to the police inspector. They also handed over the diamonds they had collected on their journey. Tahiyah and a couple of other Berbers waited in the background, offering moral support.

The inspector listened patiently while his assistant took notes. Sometimes he looked surprised; mostly he just nodded from time to time.

But at one point he frowned. They had got as far as the oasis. The inspector said a few words to one of his men, who hurried out of the hut. He came back a moment later with a map, which he unfurled on the table.

Beck and Peter looked at it with interest. They had walked across the whole area shown on this map. The inspector pointed to what was probably the wadi they had camped in, and the salt pan they had crossed. There wasn't much else on a map of the desert.

'But, see' – the inspector waved a hand right across the map – 'no oasis marked here. There is no open water south of here for two hundred miles.'

Beck frowned and leaned closer. 'There must be. It must have been about . . . here . . . no, here . . .'

But the inspector was adamant. According to the map, there was nothing that resembled an oasis anywhere near where they had been.

'We know where you found water.' Tahiyah spoke calmly and unexpectedly. 'You not find it on map.'

'What do you mean?' Peter asked.

'It is . . . special water. If your . . . ah . . .' She frowned in frustration at her limited English, and said something to Al.

He smiled, and nodded. 'The legend is that the oasis appears to those in need,' he said. 'Specifically, to those whose cause is just and whose hearts are true. And I'd say that describes you two nicely.'

Beck and Peter looked at each other, unsure what to make of this.

The inspector waved a dismissive hand. 'A legend? Who believes the old legends?'

Al looked at him with a level gaze. 'It wasn't you who was lost in the desert in need of help.'

'It could just be an oasis that the map makers didn't know about,' Peter said thoughtfully as they wandered through the village later on.

'It could be.'

But Beck thought back. He remembered the prayers he had offered up, and he remembered how Mrs Chalobah had described the smugglers. They shamed Africa. Was it so hard to believe that Africa could fight back? That good could win through?

'Here's another car coming,' Peter remarked. The dust cloud had appeared some way off as another vehicle headed towards the village.

Five minutes later it was close enough for Beck to make out a roof cluttered with what looked at first like a complicated roof rack.

'Oh, no . . .' he muttered. The roof rack was in fact a collection of aerials and satellite dishes.

The press had caught up with them. The boys stood still and watched the car approach the main hut.

'Well, this will be good practice for you. You want to be a journalist,' Beck teased Peter.

Peter frowned. 'Nah. I've had enough excitement

for a bit. Maybe I should just keep the photography as a hobby . . .'

Beck smiled. 'So what would you do instead?' he asked him.

'I dunno. Accountant maybe. That should be less dangerous. Chasing numbers instead of scorpions.'

'Well, at least we had an adventure, Pete,' Beck added with a wry smile.

'Listen, Beck, you're in danger of being the worst person on earth to go on holiday with!'

They both laughed out loud, and with their hands in their pockets they wandered towards the press jeep, where Uncle Al seemed to be in full flow, recounting the story of diamond smuggling – and desert survival by his wayward nephew, Beck Granger, and his friend.

NAVIGATING BY THE SUN

In *Sands of the Scorpion*, Beck Granger must make his way across the Sahara Desert, using the sun as a guide. Solar navigation, like astronavigation, is a time-honoured method of finding your way. There are two methods of doing this: the staff method and the watch method.

The staff method

This method works in northern temperate zones (from the Tropic of Cancer to the Arctic Circle) and southern temperate zones (from the Tropic of Capricorn to the Antarctic Circle).

Find a straight stick about a metre long and stick it in the ground where it will cast a definite shadow. Mark the point where the tip of the shadow falls (1). Wait for about 15 minutes. The shadow will move. Mark the tip of the second shadow. Draw a line from the first mark to the second mark and about 30cm beyond (2). Stand with your left foot on the first point and your right foot on the second (3).

If you are in a northern temperate zone, you are now facing approximately north; in a southern temperate zone you are facing approximately south.

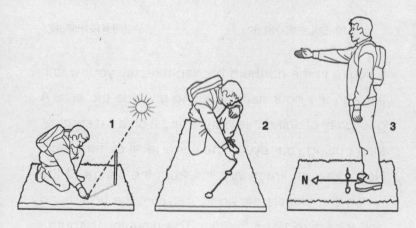

The watch method

This is a handy method of getting a rough direction, but it's not as accurate as the staff method. The closer you are to the equator, the less accurate it is.

To orientate yourself using your watch, you need to make sure it is telling the accurate local time. If a daylight-saving hour has been added, you need to wind the watch back an hour.

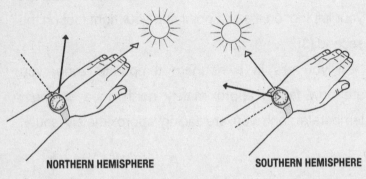

NORTHERN HEMISPHERE **SOUTHERN HEMISPHERE**

If you're in the northern hemisphere, lay your watch flat with the hour hand pointing towards the sun. A good way of doing this is by laying it on a flat surface, then putting your eye at the same level of the watch. Now, draw an imaginary line from the centre of the watch that bisects the angle between the hour hand and the figure 12 on the dial. This direction is south.

In the southern hemisphere, you need to point the figure 12 on your watch towards the sun, then bisect the angle between the hour hand and 12 o'clock. This direction is north.

ABOVE ALL, REMEMBER: NEVER, EVER GIVE UP!

BEAR GRYLLS is one of the world's most famous adventurers. After spending three years in the SAS he set off to explore the globe in search of even bigger challenges. He has climbed Mount Everest, crossed the Sahara Desert and circumnavigated Britain on a jet-ski. His TV shows have been seen by more than 1.2 billion viewers in more than 150 countries. In 2009, Bear became Chief Scout to the Scouting Association. He lives in London and Wales with his wife Shara and their three sons: Jesse, Marmaduke and Huckleberry.

Read on for a peek at the next breathtaking

MISSION☉SURVIVAL adventure,

TRACKS
OF THE TIGER...

CHAPTER ONE

The three volcanoes seemed to be moving steadily towards the rickety bus. They looked like a child's drawing – perfect cones that rose up above the Indonesian jungle for hundreds of metres. Puffs of smoke rose from the top. One was far away on the horizon, one was slightly nearer, and one was so close you had to press your face to the swaying window to see all of it.

The bus tilted as its load of tourists crowded over to one side to peer out. Beck Granger had been sitting nearest the window and he felt himself being pushed against the glass.

From the plane the jungle had looked like a sea. Its waves were the endless canopy of leaves that rose and fell with the ground beneath it. Its spray was the mists that burst out of the saturated air when it could hold no more water. Instead of fish, it was home to countless reptiles, insects and mammals. In place of sharks, crocodiles patrolled its rivers, and tigers roamed in the dark depths beneath the trees. It stretched as far as the eye could see and covered most of the island of Sumatra.

Now they were down in the jungle's heart. It was right outside the windows, rattling past at thirty miles an hour. A tangled mass of hundreds of square miles of virgin rainforest. And within it, thousands of different plant species all scrabbled for growing space. Each plant had only one objective, and that was to be slightly higher than the others so that it could reach the sky and soak up the sun's rays. The searing heat and the humidity meant that they had all the energy and water they needed. Now all they had to do was grow.

The volcanoes had been hidden by the tangle of trees and undergrowth that crowded in on either side of the bumpy road. Then the bus drove through this clearing and they just appeared. The nearest was so close you couldn't tell it was a volcano – it just looked like another mountain, until you looked more closely. The steep sides were covered in thick vegetation but wisps of smoke rose from hidden clefts in the rock. It looked like the kind of place dragons might be hiding. Beck smiled to himself at the thought, but then the smile faded.

He had visited this part of the world before. For a while he had lived with his parents in a village in Borneo. The native people had taught him how to survive in the jungle, how to live with the land rather than against it, how to find food and water and, most importantly, how to look after himself. But he had never been near an active volcano. That was something he didn't know about, but he had naturally been intrigued.

Beck knew that if you were properly prepared, there was no reason you couldn't survive . . . well, anywhere, really. But he also knew that if a volcano exploded in the wrong place, you were dead – end of story. Volcanoes were a force that humankind couldn't control and probably never would. They looked magnificent from a distance, but Beck was quietly glad that this was as close as they were going to get.

Behind him, someone breathed in awe. 'Good grief.' Mr Grey, his friend Peter's dad, was looking out of the window over Beck's shoulder. 'What a sight.'

'Dad, we've been up Vesuvius.' That was Peter in the seat beside Beck, practical and matter-of-fact.

'Yes, but you don't normally expect to be able to see three volcanoes together without even moving your head.'

The tour guide was saying much the same thing to the rest of the bus. He was a small, wiry Malay man with a big grin. The tourists listened avidly as he told them that a line of volcanic activity, known as the 'Ring of Fire', ran all around the Pacific Rim. It started in New Zealand, then ran up past Australia, through Southeast Asia, past Japan and China, then round and down past the west coasts of North and South America. Indonesia sat smack on the Ring and had over a hundred active volcanoes. Its collection included possibly the most famous of the lot, Krakatoa.